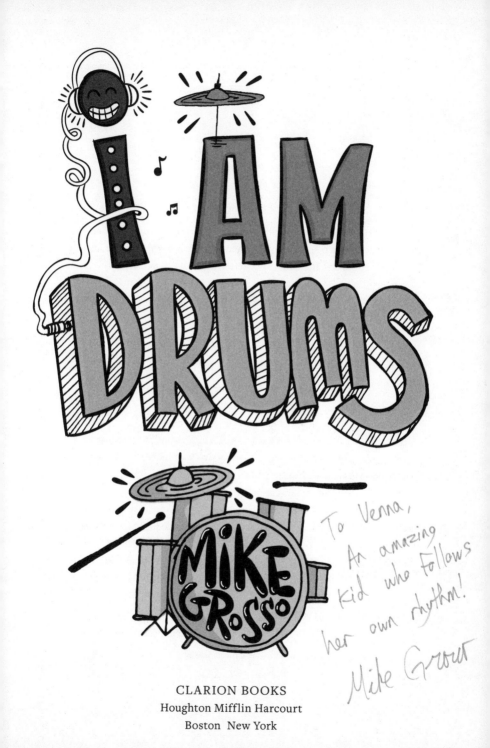

I AM DRUMS

MIKE GROSSO

To Venna,
An amazing
kid who follows
her own rhythm!

Mike Grosso

CLARION BOOKS
Houghton Mifflin Harcourt
Boston New York

Clarion Books
3 Park Avenue
New York, New York 10016

www.hmhco.com

The text was set in FreightText Book.
Design by Lisa Vega

Library of Congress Cataloging-in-Publication Data
Names: Grosso, Mike, author.
Title: I am drums / by Mike Grosso.
Description: Boston ; New York : Clarion Books, Houghton Mifflin Harcourt,
[2016] | Summary: "A single-minded twelve-year-old drummer, challenged by her
school's budget cuts and her family's financial woes, must find a way to keep her dreams
of drumming alive"—Provided by publisher.
Identifiers: LCCN 2015041139 | ISBN 9780544707108 (hardback)
Subjects: | CYAC: Drummers (Musicians)—Fiction. | Middle schools—Fiction. |
Schools—Fictoin. | Sex role—Fiction. | Interpersonal relations—Fiction. |
Family life—Fiction. | BISAC: JUVENILE FICTION / Performing Arts / Music. |
JUVENILE FICTION / School & Education. | JUVENILE FICTION / Family /
Marriage & Divorce. | JUVENILE FICTION / Girls & Women.
Classification: LCC PZ7.1.G79 Iaah 2016 | DDC [E]—dc23
LC record available at https://lccn.loc.gov/2015041139

Manufactured in the United States of America
DOC 10 9 8 7 6 5 4 3 2 1
4500608304

To Anna, because I would've stopped on page two

CHAPTER
1

If I had one wish, I'd ask for a headphone jack in my head. Not a pony, or a crazy-fast car, or a big pile of money to waste on ponies and crazy-fast cars. That kind of stuff is predictable. With a headphone jack in your head, you could let anyone plug right in and listen to your thoughts, especially the complicated stuff, like the hisses and hums in your brain. I want people to understand me when I can't say what's on my mind.

That happens to me a lot. Most days I say a ton of things that don't make sense because I don't know how to say things that do. With a headphone jack, I wouldn't have to find words to explain myself. I'd just let people plug in and listen.

One of those moments happened today, right after I hit

Danny Lenix with my marimba mallet and right before the lunch lady hauled me into the principal's office.

"Have you lost your mind?" she shouted, and grabbed the mallet out of my hand. I thought it was a rhetorical question until she said, "Say something, Sam! Explain yourself!"

All I could think to say was "I'm not sure I had my mind to begin with." Like I said, a headphone jack would be pretty handy.

"Of all the—" she said, before shaking her head and escorting me out of the lunchroom.

She brought me to the person I'm staring at now—Dr. Pullman, the tall-and-deep-voiced-to-the-point-it's-scary principal of Kennedy Middle School.

Dr. Pullman is one of those adults who shaved his head because he was too impatient to go bald. One day his head started to get a little shinier, and then . . . POW! No hair at all! The pitch-black suit he wears makes him all the more eerie.

He looks at me and says, "Take your hat off in school."

I pull the baseball cap off my head. I wear it so often, I can never remember to take it off when I enter the building.

"Can you tell me why you're here?" Dr. Pullman asks.

I know what he wants me to say. He wants me to admit that I hit Danny and I'm really sorry for doing such an awful thing and I'll never do it again. But there's more to it than that. It's like I said—if only I had that headphone jack.

"A lunch supervisor says you hit Danny with a drumstick," Dr. Pullman says.

"That's not true," I say. "I hit Danny with a mallet."

Dr. Pullman's entire head gets *seriously* red. The bottom of his chin to the top of his head is a cherry tomato. I don't know if he's mad or trying not to laugh.

"Is that supposed to be funny?" he finally says. "Do you think you're still in elementary school?"

"Danny said girls look stupid playing drums," I say, looking down at the floor. "He said girls have no rhythm and I sound like I'm playing on a garbage can because that's all my family can afford. People thought that was pretty funny."

Dr. Pullman sighs. "Well, he shouldn't have said that. But, Samantha—"

"Sam," I say, correcting him. I hate it when people call me Samantha. There's nothing wrong with the name Sam that can be fixed with an extra two syllables.

"*Sam,*" he says with emphasis.

"I was minding my own business, practicing with my mallets, and he started saying my rhythm sucks and I ruin every song in band class."

"I already said he shouldn't have said that, but you have to learn that there are other ways to solve problems that won't land you in trouble. You chose to solve your problem by hitting Danny with your mallet, and as a result, it is you in my office instead of him."

"Danny's been making fun of me all year. He acts like there's something wrong with me for playing drums."

"Plenty of girls play drums. Why would you even let that bother you?"

That's easy for Dr. Pullman to say. There are plenty of men who work at Kennedy, but I'm the only girl in the percussion section in band.

"I'm sick of him saying I stink at drums when he doesn't know anything about them."

"That still doesn't mean we solve our problems by hitting people or picking fights. You're in a bigger school now, with bigger consequences."

I nod, imagining a rubber band stretched from the top of my forehead to my chin, forcing me to bob my head in agreement.

"You'll have to serve lunch detention with me," he says, "and I'll be handing these over to Ms. Rinalli"—he holds up the mallets—"until I can trust that you will only use them for playing the timpani."

"They're not for the timpani," I say. "They're *marimba* mallets."

"Whatever they are, I'll make sure—"

"It's just that they're *really* not the same thing. Two different materials, two different sounds, and they—"

"I get the point!" he says, louder this time. There goes my mouth, getting me into even more trouble. Why can't I ever shut up?

"I'm sorry," I say. "Are you going to talk to Danny? Is he in trouble too?"

"That's between me and him. It's none of your business."

Well, then, I guess that's that. No point in saying anything else.

"As for you," he says, "you'll be coming down to my office for the next few lunch periods. And don't plan on seeing those drumsticks again until you're at band."

"Mallets," I say. "Marimba mallets."

"Whatever they are, they stay with Ms. Rinalli until further notice."

Dr. Pullman writes a few notes and gives me a hall pass to get back to class. I guess our conversation was supposed to mean something, but I'm still in trouble and Danny still made fun of me for playing drums and people still laughed. Serving a few lunch detentions with the principal won't change any of those things.

I dread going back to class. Almost everybody saw what I did, and those who didn't have probably heard about it by now. Everyone who watches me as I walk into sixth-period social studies twenty minutes late knows where I've been. The only two whose eyes don't follow me from the door to my seat are my teacher, Mrs. Pitts, and Scott, who probably feels bad for not sticking up for me at lunch.

Scott can be weird like that. He's another drummer in band, and he talks to me during rehearsal, but not so much anywhere else. It's like he crawls inside himself whenever there's a lot of people around. That's okay with me, but I wish sometimes he made it clear whether or not he actually wants to be my friend outside of band.

Danny makes a face at me as I take my seat, but I look away. I don't have anything against blond hair, but I suddenly hate that color every time I see his tangled little bowl haircut.

The rest of the period passes slowly. I spend most of it reminding myself that I don't have any other classes with Danny until band at the end of the day.

I look at Mrs. Pitts's poster that says *No one can make you feel inferior without your consent.* I can't help thinking that I do a pretty good job of making myself feel inferior without anyone else's help.

Later that day, I'm walking home with Kristen, who seems to be the only person I can stand this week. She's been my best friend ever since first grade, and even though I'm not sure she's thought of me as her best friend since elementary school, she's still cool and fun to walk home with.

We're crossing the big, noisy bridge over the Eisenhower Expressway when Kristen says, "I still can't believe you hit Danny with a mallet."

I look past the guardrail at the cars speeding underneath the bridge, passing through the town of Eastmont, and heading toward the skyline of Chicago in the distance. "He hits people all the time. Why is it such a big deal when someone hits back?"

"Probably because he was screaming like a little girl!" Kristen lets out a big laugh. I'm not proud of hitting Danny, but it's nice to know someone appreciated it.

"Yeah, well, I'm totally grounded for it," I say. "As soon as my parents get home and hear Dr. Pullman's message, I'll be imprisoned in my room for the rest of my life."

Kristen sighs. "What about my pool party? They'll let you out for that, right?"

I shrug. "It's not for another two months, so my dad should be cooled down by then."

"You've been there every year since first grade, Sam! You have to come."

"I'll be there. My dad can't stay mad forever."

Kristen looks at the ground as we walk side by side. "You didn't need to hit him."

"I know."

"Nobody cares what Danny says."

"Then why were they all laughing?" *And why were you laughing with them?* I think but can't bring myself to say aloud.

Even Kristen, one of the smartest people I know, doesn't have an answer for that. I don't think anybody does. She's not shy like Scott, and she's known me much longer. She could have stood up for me.

We're well past the bridge over the Eisenhower Expressway and walking by Silverlight Jewelers. I look in the window at glowing necklaces and bracelets, imagining the price tags.

Later we're passing numerous houses and trees when we hear the sounds of beating and banging. They fill my ears as we approach a familiar brown house at the end of a long block. The sounds are like candy. I can't explain it without that headphone jack—how else can you describe sounds so amazing they give you chills just thinking about them?

"I hate walking by Pete Taylor's house," Kristen says. "It's so obnoxious."

"I think it's awesome," I say. "Is it true that Pete has two full drum sets?"

"Why would I know? I can't think of anything more boring."

I listen to the clashing sounds of snares and cymbals bleeding through the basement windows. "I wish I could take private lessons."

"Why?"

"I like drums. Scott says he's the best teacher in town."

Kristen gives me a weird look. As cool as she is, she can certainly act just like everyone else sometimes. Is it really that weird for a girl to play drums?

"Why don't you just ring the doorbell and ask Pete to give you lessons?" she asks.

"My parents wouldn't pay for it," I say. "Did you know he charges thirty dollars for a half hour?"

"How'd you find that out?"

"I called his house once, pretending to be my mom. Pete gave me the cold shoulder, saying he's overbooked already. No room to take on a new student."

Kristen opens her mouth to say something else but stops short. "Sorry."

I shrug as we keep walking, the perfect blend of rhythmic craziness disappearing behind us. We don't talk much for the rest of the way home. Kristen spends most of it playing with her hair—she's letting it grow long this year. It's a much brighter shade of brown than mine, which is so dark it almost looks black. I've tried to let it grow out, but it doesn't seem to want to go past my jaw.

Suddenly, I say, "Do you think what Danny said was funny?"

Kristen stops walking and turns toward me. "I don't think anything that idiot says is funny. Anyone that thinks he's funny is a moron."

I want to say thanks, but I can't get the image of her laughing out of my head.

CHAPTER 2

My parents still own an encyclopedia. A real encyclopedia, not something you find online that claims Bigfoot invented the lightbulb. I'm talking about a collection of four-hundred-pound books full of stuff you never wanted to know until your teacher assigned a research paper about it. I'm glad my parents still have them, because they make a solid *THUMP* that's perfect for the sound of toms, the drums mounted on top of the bass drum. They meld flawlessly with an old, falling-apart Calvin and Hobbes book that I use as a snare—it's a paperback, so it makes a nice, high-pitched *THWAP* when I hit it. A huge—and I mean *really* huge—dictionary is my bass drum, so I put it on the floor under my computer desk and stomp it with my Converse All Stars whenever I need a thick *WHOMP*.

My computer desk is kind of funny, because it doesn't have a computer on it. My parents call it a homework desk to make me feel better about my lack of a computer, which seems totally lame to me, even if it is a pretty good place to do homework. It beats working in the kitchen, where my younger brother, Brian, complains nonstop about how much homework third-graders get.

Whenever I go near Brian, he says, "Stop staring at me."

And I say, "I'm not staring at you."

"Can you see me right now?"

"Yes."

"How could you see me unless you're staring at me?"

"If I was staring at you, my eyeballs would be on fire."

"Mom! Sam's staring at me!"

It's all downhill from there.

I've been calling my computer/homework desk my drum desk for five years, ever since I saw a drum solo by John Bonham from Led Zeppelin in an old music documentary. My brain exploded as his arms flew across the kit during the song "Moby Dick." I went online and researched each piece of a standard drum set that night, memorizing the purpose and setup for each one.

I learned the hi-hat is two cymbals that clamp together when the drummer presses a pedal, and the crash cymbal sounds just like its name, and the snare is the backbeat in rock music because it sounds like someone getting punched in the face in a martial arts movie.

I told my dad about the John Bonham video and asked if he liked Led Zeppelin when he was younger. He laughed and said, "Would you still like him if I told you he died from drinking vodka for twelve hours straight?"

I didn't know how to respond. I get what he was trying to say, but it's not like playing drums and having an alcohol problem are the same thing.

My desk set has two levels, so I put the encyclopedia toms and the Calvin and Hobbes snare on the lower level. I pull the latest edition of the *Chicago Tribune* out of the recycling bin and put that on the top shelf. The big fat Sunday paper is my crash cymbal, and the Monday and Tuesday papers are my ride and hi-hat. This is my homemade drum set—the only set my family can afford. And I make it work pretty well, thank you very much, even if it just makes me imagine the real thing. Sometimes I put earplugs in to dampen the noise and make it sound thicker. If I hit as hard as I can, I can almost hear what it would be like if I was rocking out on a real set. That's usually when someone barges into my room and tells me to knock it off.

I can't exactly blame them. It's not a real drum set, so it can't be pleasant to listen to. I taught myself enough to get placed in Kennedy's symphonic band earlier this year instead of beginning concert band, but I know that's not saying much. It's hard to get good at something all on your own.

Today is nice, because no one's home yet, and I've been rocking out for a full twenty minutes when a thought enters my mind.

Listen to the message. Find out what Dr. Pullman said so you can at least have an idea of how bad it's going to be.

I stand up from my drum desk and walk downstairs, the wooden steps creaking and the railing rattling. I pick up the phone and listen for the double click of the dial tone that confirms there is a new message. I punch in the four-digit password and hit 1 to hear new messages, and I hear Dr. Pullman's voice:

Hello, Mr. and Mrs. Morris. This is Daniel Pullman from Kennedy Middle School calling about a lunchroom incident this afternoon that involved your daughter. Please call me back whenever it is convenient to do so. I can be reached at—

Dr. Pullman rattles off a number, but I'm not really listening. He wants to have a personal conversation with my mom and dad. That's not good. They'll be mad just for being inconvenienced. Not my mom so much, but my dad—oh, man, you don't want him mad. You pretty much lose every privilege you can imagine, even if it's only a little bit your fault. Even if you just lost control for a split second.

Even if you felt totally humiliated.

There's a loud beep, signaling that Dr. Pullman's message is over, followed by a computerized female voice that says, *"Press seven to save this message. Press nine to delete this message."*

I pull the phone away from my ear and try to come up with a way to explain this to my dad. I don't want him any madder at me than he already is. He's spent the whole school year fielding calls about how I'm falling behind and not taking middle school seriously and how I still think I'm a fifth-grader or something. It's late March—a little over two months from now, it will be summer, and I will be free from the pressure and agony of school. Free to enjoy Kristen's annual pool party in early June and a summer full of wild, crazy fun after that. Can't I manage to make it two more months without getting into more trouble with my dad?

The computerized voice says, *"Please make a selection.*

Press seven to save this message. Press nine to delete this message."

My hand shakes, but I slowly bring my index finger down. It lands on the number 9.

"Your message has been deleted."

I hang up the phone and run back upstairs, trying to forget the message ever existed, because as far as anyone besides me and Dr. Pullman knows, it never really did.

CHAPTER 3

"Sam?" my mom says.

I gaze into my bagel, my eyes struggling to stay open as they trace the knife lines of cream cheese. The second hand on the wall clock ticks, and in my head a million other household items tap along, blending into one imaginary percussive orchestra.

"Sam!" my mom shouts, and my body jumps into alertness to find her staring me down like a wild animal.

"What?" I say.

"I said your name three times."

"Sorry. Can't I eat my bagel in peace?"

"You need to listen better."

I slump my shoulders. "I'm just tired this morning."

"Then you need to go to bed earlier."

Sure, Mom. I'll just fall asleep earlier. I'll tell my mind to stop dreaming of drums, and the tossing and turning in the middle of the night while giant pounding rhythms play in my head will magically disappear. I'll never be distracted by sleep again.

"I'm having trouble sleeping," I say.

"Why?" she asks. "Is something the matter?"

"I don't know. No, not really. I'm just thinking a lot."

"You're such a dreamer."

You want to know what's weird about being called a dreamer? Each person who says it means something different. It's hard to tell sometimes if it's an insult—are they admiring you or making fun of you for being naïve?

My mom calls me a dreamer constantly, but not in a mean way. It's like she admires me and feels sorry for me at the same time. She's waiting for the sky to fall so she can tell me how silly I am for not realizing such a thing could happen. *Poor Sam. She doesn't even realize the world is collapsing all around her.*

My dad is another story. Lately he's kind of like a ticking time bomb. He can be totally okay, and then *BOOM!* He explodes at the slightest bother. I love him and all, but it's hard sometimes to know what's going to set him off.

My father walks into the kitchen, tying his tie as he grumbles to himself.

"Why doesn't this shirt ever iron right?" he says.

"Because you don't know how to iron," my mom says.

"I know how to iron just fine. It's because the iron needs to be replaced."

He fidgets with his tie for a few minutes before my mom comes over and says, "Calm down and let me help." She grabs both ends of his tie and starts crossing and looping until a perfect knot is formed.

"It's not like I don't know how to do it," my dad says.

"Sure, honey," my mom says.

My dad watches my mom's hands as they adjust his collar. "You still haven't found it?" he asks.

My mom shakes her head. Her wedding ring went missing several days ago, and my dad is trying hard not to be upset about it. He knows how bad my mom feels.

"I can keep an eye out for it," I say.

"Thanks, Sam. I'm sure it'll turn up soon." But the look on her face tells me she's not so sure.

"And you, Sam," my dad says, pointing at me like I've personally offended him, "you'd better be ready in five minutes. You're not making me late for work again."

"She didn't make you late, honey," my mom says.

My dad takes a breath, scratches his head, and says, "I know. I just need to get there early today. No dawdling, Sam. I mean it! Be ready in five minutes!"

I tell him I will be, but he only waits two minutes before he starts losing his mind and saying, "I told you to be ready in five minutes!"

I consider correcting him before remembering that he doesn't respond well to back talk, especially when he's already stressed. Sometimes I wonder if even that headphone jack could help me with my father.

"Just go to work, Dale," my mom says. "I'll take her."

My dad scoffs, grabs his keys, and leaves without saying goodbye. My mom just sighs and says, "Take your time, honey." When I don't say anything in response, she says, "He's under a lot of stress. The new job isn't exactly what they told him it would be."

"I know," I say.

I don't really blame my dad for being in a twenty-four-hour bad mood the last few months. He lost his job last year, so my parents were making ends meet on Mom's small salary and Dad's even smaller unemployment check until he finally landed a new job a couple of months ago. He barely makes half of what he used to and hates what he does, but Mom and Dad seem unsure what else to do.

That's why I only asked for a drum set once. And I had the miserable luck of asking for it the day my dad came home with the news that he'd been laid off. He totally blew a gasket when I asked. It was like I was the one who'd lost his job.

Great timing, Sam.

My mom and I head into the garage and jump inside the old Caravan. The engine makes a weird whistling noise and the tires wobble a bit, but it gets us where we want to go.

"Can I ask you something, Sam?" my mom says.

"I guess," I say.

"How do all those books on your desk work?"

Chills run up my spine. The mention of my desk set gets me all defensive. I feel like a four-year-old playing pretend. "Why are you asking?"

"I don't know. Mothers are curious by nature."

"It's just a way to practice."

My mom glances toward me and smiles. "Practice what? Your drum parts for the school band?"

My throat clenches, the top and bottom sticking together as everything goes dry. Why is it so hard to talk to her about this? Maybe because my mom doesn't understand that it's about more than just my parts for the school band.

Maybe because drums shouldn't disappear when the school bell rings.

Maybe because I'm worried I'll never be any good without a real kit and a teacher who isn't distracted by sixty other students.

Maybe because the last time I talked to my parents about drums, my dad freaked out because he'd just lost his job and didn't want his daughter to have an "expensive hobby."

When I don't answer, my mom looks offended and says, "I'm just asking a question."

"I just mess around," I say quickly. "It's not a big deal."

She's quiet as a tomb for a few more seconds before speaking again. "You don't need to be embarrassed, Sam. You can be whatever you want to be. The sky's the limit."

I nod as if I understand, but it's not that simple. If she was truly okay with the person I want to be, I wouldn't be drumming on Calvin and Hobbes, afraid to tell her the truth about the rhythms in my head that won't let me sleep at night.

I can't help noticing the indentation in her ring finger as it curls around the steering wheel. It's like someone else's finger without that plain gold band on it. It wasn't fancy or anything, but something about a missing wedding ring makes me sad.

"Will it cost a lot to replace?" I ask.

"You don't need to worry about that," she says, "but yes, it will."

That's a nice way of saying *replacement* isn't an option.

The rest of the car ride feels longer than it ever has before.

Today isn't all bad, though. I manage to show up early for once, drop my things off at my locker in the sixth-grade wing, and sneak down to the music room as I sometimes do to ogle the instruments while the room is empty.

This morning, however, the room is most certainly *not* empty.

There's a band rehearsing. I snag an empty chair just inside the music room where the clarinets sit and watch a group of seventh- and eighth-graders who make up Kennedy's jazz band. There are trumpets, saxophones, flutes, and trombones. I'm thrilled to see there is one guy in the back playing the sousaphone, the biggest instrument I've ever seen. It's like a gigantic tuba that wraps around his whole body before ending in a black hole atop his head where a low-pitched *honk* comes out.

Next to him is an eighth-grader sitting at our school's piano. He's the only nonteacher allowed to even touch it, much less play it. I swear he's playing all eighty-eight keys at once.

The Kennedy jazz band is the almighty pinnacle of middle school music. I heard them play a few times earlier in the year, and I've been waiting for my chance to audition ever since. They sound even better now. I haven't heard a lot of jazz, but I know what it sounds like and can spot a few things about it. The music they play isn't really jazz, but I guess you could call it that if you wanted to. It's all rock songs redone with swingy beats. I like it. It has so much more energy than the songs we play in the symphonic band and some of the craziest rhythms I've ever heard. Plus, it's the only school music program that uses a full drum set. Every other music program cuts percussion into pieces. *You want to play the set, eh? Why don't you just play snare instead? Or hit a cymbal once every three hours?* It's cruel and unusual punishment for someone like me.

There's a bass player on the left side of the group, and he's not playing one of those big acoustic upright basses. He has an electric bass! He's grooving in perfect time with the drums.

Yes! The drums!

The Holy Grail of school music programs! It has everything—crash and ride cymbals, a hi-hat that isn't totally broken, a snare, three toms, and a big fat bass drum. A tall guy is sitting on the throne. Johnny Parker, king of drums at

Kennedy Middle School. He has dark hair that's wavy all over except in the front, where he spikes it up. I imagine myself in his place, behind the kit, landing every beat and fill in perfect time.

I listen to their rehearsal and feel my stomach vibrate each time the rhythm kicks in. The horns blare the melody. The bass swings the band along. And the drums twist and writhe and wiggle their way through the song. I don't even know if I like the song itself, but man, do I love listening to it. So many instruments and so much noise.

And there's a full drum set. I really want to join a band where I get to play one. My desk set at home seems so lame when I'm watching people more talented than I'll ever be go to town on their instruments.

They finish playing, and the students start storming out of the room. I sit quietly and pretend to be uninterested, all the while hoping no one notices the big dork who wishes she could be sitting behind the drum kit.

"You're Sam," a voice says.

I spin around and see a familiar girl's face staring at me, surprised and intrigued at the same time. She carries a trumpet. She's tall enough to be an eighth-grader, easily.

"My little brother knows you," she says. "You're in symphonic band together."

That's when it clicks why she's so familiar. "You're Scott's sister!" I say, trying not to sound too excited. I can't believe I didn't realize it earlier—they look almost exactly the same, except for the obvious. "You're Jessica! Scott never told me you played the trumpet in jazz band!"

"That's me."

"Cool. I tried the trumpet once, but it just sounded like bad gas." *Oh my God, Sam! Please just shut up!*

But Jessica gives a small chuckle, and I feel a little better about my silly joke. "Are you joining jazz band?"

"Um," I say, not knowing what to say.

"Oh, wait," she says. "You're still in sixth grade. Can't audition until next year."

"Yeah," I say. "And anyways, I want to join as a drummer. That's a little weird, I know."

"Why is that weird?"

I freeze up. I thought it was obvious. "Well, you know. Being a girl, and all."

"Not a lot of girls play trumpet either," Jessica says. "Except they do, because I said they do. Just something to think about." Then Jessica waves goodbye and says, "Keep my brother in line, okay?" She starts to take her trumpet apart to pack it up.

Talking with Jessica gives me a new burst of courage.

My eyes turn to Johnny Parker. He's busy breaking down the drum set, collapsing cymbals and stands and putting the toms into bags. I take a deep breath and try to think of something really clever to say as I approach him—something that will make me sound like a real musician. The best I can come up with is "Do you need any help?"

He stops, gives me a shocked look, and shakes his head. Not a word in response.

"I'm not trying to interrupt. I just wanted to let you know that you sound awesome on the drums."

"Um, yeah, I know," he says.

"*Really* good."

"Yeah, I already said I know."

He starts giving me this look. It's the kind of look adults give to three-year-olds. I'm not liking it.

"How did you learn to play?" I ask.

"Private lessons and a lot of natural skill. I've always had a top-notch sense of rhythm."

Private lessons. How I wish I had those. There's only so much you can learn by yourself. And even though I know it's going to hurt to hear the answer, I ask anyway. "Who gives you lessons?"

"The same teacher every good drummer goes to," he says. "Pete Taylor."

Pete Taylor. Why did it have to be him? The coolest music teacher, with the coolest house and the coolest sounds coming out of the coolest basement. Not that I've seen his basement before, but I swear it has to be the greatest thing I've never seen. I wonder if Johnny knows how lucky he is.

"Is there something else you need?" Johnny asks, starting to look impatient.

"I play drums too," I say. I'm really proud to say it until Johnny starts laughing his head off, like I just said the funniest thing he's ever heard in his life. Jessica must hear him, because she looks in our direction.

"Keep up the hard work," he says, obviously being sarcastic.

"What's that supposed to mean?"

"Nothing. Just forget it."

"Is there a problem?" Jessica says from behind me. I turn around and see her, trumpet mouthpiece in her hand, clenched a bit too tight.

"Of course not!" Johnny says, though his tone makes it clear there is definitely something wrong. "Now leave me alone so I can finish packing these up."

Jessica is about to respond, but I stop her. "It's okay. I was just telling him that I enjoyed his drumming."

"I hope he listened," Jessica says, "because you're going to take his spot next year."

"Whatever you say," Johnny says. "It's just that, well, none of the girls in the drum section are very good."

I feel a hot rush, like a flaming bee sting running through me. I'm not mad at Johnny. Just hurt. *Really* hurt. He couldn't have meant it.

"Some of them have to be good," I mumble.

"Maybe they are, maybe they aren't," he says. "I was just kidding, anyways. Seriously, though? None of them made jazz band, and none of them ever will."

"Then maybe I'll be the first to change that."

"Yeah, whatever." Johnny shrugs, turns to Jessica, and says, "See you in science class, Jess. And good luck with the drums, Sarah."

"It's *Sam*," I say.

"Whatever, Sam."

Jessica says nothing else. She gives me a sympathetic look and returns to packing up her trumpet.

I'm about to leave when Ms. Rinalli taps me on the shoulder. I turn to see her standing next to me with a slight grin. "Thinking of trying out next year, Samantha?"

"It's Sam," I say, wishing a second later I'd resisted

correcting her. Stubbornness isn't going to get me into jazz band.

Thankfully, Ms. Rinalli doesn't take offense. She says, "If you can develop your drumming chops by seventh grade, I'll call you whatever you want."

She tells me to get to class and leaves my side as quickly as she appeared. Is it really possible? Could I make it into jazz band next year? It's only a matter of time until I get a chance to truly show Ms. Rinalli what I can do, which admittedly isn't much. The drumbeats in my head are so much better than what I can play on my desk set. Another reason why I wish I had that headphone jack.

CHAPTER
4

I can hardly wait to talk to Scott. I'm excited enough that I manage to forget about Johnny Parker for most of the morning before arriving at the lunch table. I find a seat next to Scott and away from Danny.

"I met your sister today," I say.

I expect him to be at least a little surprised, so it's an extra bummer when he casually says, "She told me. I ran into her before lunch."

"She's pretty cool."

"She's cool if she's not your sister. All she does is boss me around."

"You never told me she played the trumpet in jazz band."

Scott just shrugs and stares at his lunch, which looks unappetizing as usual.

We're both quiet for a few seconds while I try to think of something else to say. If I don't make Scott talk, he'll spend the entirety of lunch staring into his sandwich, pretending the rest of the world doesn't exist. He's a good friend, but he gets really nervous in crowded places, especially the lunch table. That's probably why I never see him outside of school.

Scott looks down the table at Danny, who's totally distracted by whatever cronies he's blabbing to.

"Don't worry," I say. "I'm not going to start anything with him today."

"It's not you I'm worried about," Scott says.

I try to change the subject to something more comfortable. "Are you interested in jazz band? Considering your sister is in it and all?"

He shrugs and says, "I heard it's way too hard. Not interested."

"What about Zeke?" Zeke is another drummer in band. He's really friendly, but he does seem to spend more time giggling than actually playing the drums. Out of all the kids in band, he's the most likely to show up to school dressed as a clown.

"Zeke might join if it gets him out of math next year."

Danny is apparently listening to us, because he starts shouting across the table, "The sax players in jazz band suck! The only ones worse are the trumpet players!"

I clench my fists but keep my mouth shut. He's just trying to get a rise out of us. I won't let him get me into trouble again.

Scott, the calm and quiet one, for once doesn't seem capable of this. The comment about the trumpet players must have set him off, because he shouts, "Go stick your saxophone in a toilet! It would probably sound better!"

The table erupts with laughter. Danny scowls and says, "Whatever. Have fun talking to your girlfriend. Or is that your pet ape?"

I grab Scott's hand before he can smash his sandwich inside it. "He's not worth it," I say, and hold tight as Scott settles down and resumes eating his lunch.

I give Scott a smile and receive a small, embarrassed one in return. That's Scott for you. At times he doesn't want anyone to know what he's feeling. One second he's complaining about his bossy sister, and the next he's defending her honor at the sixth-grade lunch table. At least he's not freaking out about sitting next to me after Danny's comment.

Danny wasn't always this way. He was a pretty cool kid in elementary school. He wasn't my best friend or anything, but we played with some of the same kids at recess. We also had a lot of fun whenever we worked as partners in fifth-grade science, which we were both equally bad at. Sixth grade changed a lot of that, and I'm not sure why.

I'm almost finished with my lunch when a very large black suit appears next to our lunch table.

"Can I talk to you, Samantha?" Dr. Pullman says in that awful deep voice.

"Sam," I say, but I get the worst evil eye imaginable and stand up without another word. I catch Danny giggling as I walk to the end of the lunchroom, right next to the principal.

"You were supposed to be in lunch detention today," Dr. Pullman says.

Was that today? He never told me the specific days. "I didn't know those had already started."

"They have," he says. "Do you understand how serious this is?"

I nod.

"Then don't try to skip out tomorrow, or the consequences will be worse." Dr. Pullman folds his arms. "I left a voice mail for your parents yesterday. I'm still waiting to hear back from them."

I swallow hard. "They're pretty busy lately. My dad has

a tough new job. He works late most days of the week. Even Saturdays now."

"Did they receive the message?"

My voice wavers as I say, "I'll make sure to ask them."

"I'd appreciate that." Dr. Pullman unfolds his arms and gives me another stern look. "I expect to see you in my office this time tomorrow. The moment the bell rings, and not a second later."

Dr. Pullman seems to walk away in slow motion. My throat is dry, and the hairs on my arms are like quills. What am I going to do about that erased message?

So much has happened today that it doesn't really hit me how mean Johnny Parker was after jazz rehearsal until I'm doing my homework that night. I'm sitting at my drum desk, going through mixed numbers and ratios, when I say, out loud, "You know what? You're not awesome!

"In fact," I continue, talking aloud to the wall, "you play the drums like a baboon! I'm surprised you didn't drool all over the snare drum!" And even though I'm pretty sure baboons don't drool any more than humans do, I am entirely sure this describes Johnny Parker to a T.

I remember what he said about no girls ever making it

into jazz band. If I could prove him wrong, I'd be the first girl ever on the drums. How weird is that?

Not that I've ever played jazz. I haven't even heard much of it. But the middle school jazz band brought the house down this morning, and that was only their rehearsal. Imagine what their live performance must be like. They have a full set! Everyone who makes it in is serious about their craft, like Jessica on the trumpet. It isn't like symphonic band, where half the kids just want an extra period to goof off. I'd play any style they wanted just to get a chance to rock out on a real set with serious players instead of on a stupid desk to a crowd of nobody.

Jazz band is the perfect opportunity.

CHAPTER
5

The next morning, my dad is in a really good mood. He has breakfast ready for all of us—me, Brian, and my mom—when we get downstairs. He slips some eggs and bacon onto my plate as he gives me a peck on the head and says, "I'm sorry I've been such a grouch lately. I love you guys."

I want to plug him right into my headphone jack, right there, and let him hear what happens to my heart when he says things like that. And then I want him to hear that I'm scared he'll be a grouch all over again by dinnertime.

That's the thing about my dad. He can be so angry or so nice, but it's hard to know which one he'll be at any given time. An olive can look a lot like a grape until you bite into it and want to barf from the taste.

School starts out great. I have all my homework done for a change, so I get to show up to every class without being afraid of a lecture. I remember to head to Dr. Pullman's office for my first lunch detention and even make it on time. It's not as bad as I was expecting—a lot of class work I need to catch up on and an eerie silence from Dr. Pullman, sitting behind his computer and typing away the whole time. The only bad part is at the end of lunch, when he says, "See you tomorrow." Apparently I'm not out of the woods yet.

When I show up to symphonic band, our final period of the day, we're scheduled to practice all of my favorite pieces.

The band room is an interesting place during that final period. There's sixty-plus kids with instruments at their sides crammed into a rehearsal room made for about forty.

I'm lucky enough to be in the percussion section. It can get boring when the band is practicing a song you're not scheduled to play, but at least I get to talk with the other drummers. I like Scott and Zeke the best. Scott becomes a different person back here. He actually talks without being spoken to first. It did take a while—he didn't talk to anybody the first few months. Mostly he just slept in one of the chairs, until earlier this year when Zeke woke him up by crashing cymbals an inch from his ear. They somehow became best friends after that.

Zeke is kind of bizarre, but in a hilarious way. That's more than I can say about Danny Lenix, who sits pleasantly far away from me in the saxophone section.

Danny and I participated in the same instrument fitting last year when the band teacher before Ms. Rinalli visited our elementary school. Kids interested in band took turns heading to the music room to try out several instruments. Danny was pretty excited about percussion beforehand, but he ended up liking the saxophone instead.

When my turn came to head to the music room, the teacher made me try a bunch of instruments just to be sure I wasn't missing out on any hidden talents. Maybe she wanted me to fall in love with a surprise instrument like Danny, but I knew the other instruments were wrong for me the moment I held them. I told her I loved John Bonham and wanted to be in the percussion section, so she gave me a simple rhythm test. It wasn't too complicated—she made sure I could count to four and play basic quarter and eighth notes. Every kid in the percussion section had to pass it.

"I'm bored," Scott says.

"You're always bored," I say back, because he always is.

"That's because I don't get to play anything."

Zeke and I are both thinking, *You never want to play anything.*

"You should pee in the timpani," Zeke says.

"That's nasty," Scott says, making a sour face.

"You're nasty. That's why you should do it."

"You guys are weird," I say, and they both look at me for a few seconds and resume their conversation. It's weird the way they look at me—like I'm another boy. That's something you learn quickly when you're the girl in the percussion section—you don't get to be a girl when you're playing drums.

"I would totally pee in the timpani," Zeke says.

"*How* exactly would you pee in the timpani?" I ask.

Zeke looks at me, dumbfounded, so I add, "The only way to pee inside the timpani is to take off the drum head, and I'm betting you don't have a drum key to get that done."

"I'd steal Ms. Rinalli's drum key," Zeke says.

"Even if you knew where it was—which you don't—you'd have to stand up to steal it, and good luck doing that without Ms. Rinalli seeing you."

Zeke shrugs and then says, "I would still pee in it."

"I would still pee on your head," Scott says. Like I said, it's weird how much he opens up when we're in the drum section. It's like he's safe to be himself here.

"Both of you be quiet," I say.

"Why don't you pee on something, Sam?" Zeke asks.

"Smell your bag," I say.

For a second, he's almost going to do it. Then Scott and I laugh, and he waves us away like he knew the whole time. He's pretty gullible for a self-described prankster.

But you want to know something crazy? I really like these guys. Not in a weird way or anything. I just like being around them—it makes the time spent waiting to play more bearable.

The band stops playing as the current piece ends. Ms. Rinalli announces the next song, and the class starts shuffling papers, searching for the right sheet music.

"You're up, Sam," Zeke says. "You're on the marimba."

Finally! It's never a good idea to have too much downtime, or Ms. Rinalli might think you're one of her time wasters—a kid who joins band to get out of class. The percussion section is full of them.

That's when I panic. Dr. Pullman gave my marimba mallets to Ms. Rinalli. Unless I try hitting the marimba with my head, I can't play my part without them.

I raise a nervous, shaking hand.

"Yes, Sam?" Ms. Rinalli says.

I don't know what to say. If I remind her that she has my mallets, the entire room of sixty-plus music students will know they were confiscated by the principal. It will only be a matter of time before kids from every section start mumbling about why.

"You have my marimba mallets," I say, hating myself as I do it. I catch Danny smirking over in the sax section. *Please, please, please don't make me say why in front of the entire class!*

Ms. Rinalli sighs and says, "They're in the bin in my office. Go grab them while the rest of us get started."

I breathe a sigh of relief. *Get a pair of marimba mallets out of her office.* Seems straightforward enough. It's right behind the conductor's podium, at the front of the rehearsal room. Her office is the size of a Porta-Potty, so finding anything in there should be easy.

What I don't think about, because I never think about things like this, is how I'm going to get out of the percussion section. It seems so simple, but we rehearse in a room that is not designed for sixty kids, some of them with tubas the size of Great Danes. Everyone is starting the song without me, so I can't exactly tap them on the shoulder and ask them to move. So I do what any kid might do—I tiptoe as carefully as I can between people and instruments in an attempt to get through the crowd and over to Ms. Rinalli's office.

I don't know how it happens. Some part of my arm—

probably my elbow—bumps into a flute. A shrill tweet pierces the air, followed by the sound of another kid shouting "ouch!" as she clenches her bloody lip.

My drumsticks fall out of my back pocket. I didn't even know I had them. I would have left them in the drum section if I'd remembered. My right foot slips on one of them, sending my whole body forward. I collapse into the saxophone section, right into Danny Lenix himself, and together we domino into the trombones, whose long tubes stab the woodwinds in the backs of their heads.

Within seconds, the entire band is in chaos, and I've personally assaulted kids from almost every instrument classification.

"What is wrong with you?" Danny says from the bottom of a crumpled pile of saxophone players splayed on the floor.

I stand up and survey the staring faces and damage I've caused. I nervously smile back, as if somehow that will affirm my innocence and keep me out of trouble for taking out half of the band.

Ms. Rinalli sees me standing in the middle of musical wreckage, freaked out, surrounded by shoved and squished kids with instruments wedged in their faces.

"In my office, Samantha!" Ms. Rinalli says. "Now! We'll talk after class!"

I don't even bother telling her to call me *Sam*. I slump my shoulders and pick up my sticks to bring with me.

"Leave the sticks here!"

Man! I really wanted them with me. It's so boring sitting in there with nothing to do.

I walk all the way behind the podium and into Ms. Rinalli's office—a closet-size space with stacks of sheet music and half-destroyed instruments. I get sent here a lot, especially when I'm in the middle of playing. I don't know how, but I think I get in trouble more often when I have more band responsibility.

I shut the door behind me and listen as the sound of rehearsal muffles. There used to be a few cellos and an upright bass squeezed into this little space that I used to mess around with, but Ms. Rinalli caught me plucking the strings and put them in another room. Now there's nothing but me and four walls and the dampened sound of the band in the classroom outside. It sucks pretty bad. Zeke is the only one who gets put in here more often than me, and he just falls asleep. I don't know how anyone can fall asleep when there's music playing.

It's weird, too, because it's not like I get put in here because I want to goof off. I take band seriously. I really do. It's just that I'm not sure it's the kind of seriousness people talk about in all the other classes. I mean, are we really supposed to sit still in those plastic chairs and be silent when it's not our turn to play? And when it *is* our turn, do we always have to play the notes on the page? What if I come up with a better part? What if there's a better beat, or a better rhythm? And what if it really is better and it's not just me being a brat and wanting to do things my own way all the time?

Isn't it possible that a dreamer like me might actually know what she's talking about every once in a while?

Twenty minutes later, the walls of Ms. Rinalli's office are darker, and the band is gone. I stay still. I learned the hard way that when certain teachers tell you to stay put, you do exactly what they asked until you're released.

I'm sitting in the one chair Ms. Rinalli keeps in her office, waiting for her to come get me and tell me that the "Planet of the Apes"—her nickname for the percussion section—has been released and I'm free to head to my locker and leave for the day.

But no one comes to get me. And that's when I hear the sound of something that scares the crap out of me like I never thought possible. Someone crying. It's Ms. Rinalli.

Now I'm *really* scared to leave. I have no idea what Ms.

Rinalli will do if she finds out I'm still here. Walking in on a teacher crying is like walking into the wrong bathroom. You just don't do it. Not even as a joke.

I hear the door to the rehearsal room open. Someone else is in here with Ms. Rinalli.

"I'm sorry, Grace," a deep male voice says. It sounds like another teacher. "I heard about the board's decision."

"They're letting all first-year teachers go," Ms. Rinalli says. "That includes me."

"It's just budget cuts," the man says. "It's nothing personal. Everyone here wants you to stay. They're probably going to call you back over the summer when they get updated enrollment numbers."

"No, Phil. They won't."

"Of course they will. They always do."

I can hear Ms. Rinalli let out a sigh. "You don't get it. They're cutting the whole program."

Cutting the program? What program? What is Ms. Rinalli talking about?

"They can't do that," the man says.

"They already have," Ms. Rinalli says. "I was just informed during lunch. Come next year, there will be no music program at Kennedy. Not at any of the middle schools."

Within seconds I feel like I'm going to burst. A tear leaves my eye, and it takes everything in me to keep from sobbing.

My heart falls into my chest. I start to sweat. My skin crawls with goose bumps and my chest feels like it's going to explode.

They're cutting the music program. When I return to Kennedy Middle School as a seventh-grader next year, there will be no music classes.

There will be no symphonic band.

There will be no orchestra or jazz band.

And there will definitely be no full drum set.

CHAPTER
6

Even though the only thing worse than crying at school is getting caught crying at school, I just can't help it. The tears fall. And when it gets so bad that I can't even bear to fight back, I start sobbing.

As soon as I start crying, Ms. Rinalli stops. The man she was speaking with has gone quiet as well. They heard me.

"Oh no," Ms. Rinalli says. "Samantha."

"You have a student in your office?" the man asks, surprised.

The door to her office opens, and I cover my face in my hands. I see Ms. Rinalli's shadow through the cracks of my fingers as she approaches and says, "Are you okay, Sam?"

Sam. She remembered to call me Sam.

"It's nothing," I say, my voice muffled by my hands. "I'm fine."

"I'll take care of this," Ms. Rinalli says to the man.

I hear the heavy footsteps of the man leaving. I see Ms. Rinalli through the cracks of my fingers, coming closer and grabbing a folding chair from the corner and placing it on the floor next to me. I finally take my hands off my face to see her with a box of tissues in her hand. She pulls one out and offers it to me. When I don't accept it, she crumples it up and puts it in her pocket.

"Are you upset that you had to sit in my office today?" she asks.

"No," I say, and even though I was at one point, it seems pretty meaningless right now.

"Do you know the social worker here at Kennedy Middle School?" she asks.

"No," I say, annoying myself with my redundant, one-word answers. The truth is I know exactly who the social worker is. I went to see him a few times at the beginning of the year when I was having trouble turning in my homework on time. His office is the last place I want to be right now.

"If you're not comfortable telling me why you're upset, there are other adults you can talk to."

"I don't want to talk to anyone."

"Then is there anything else I can do to help?"

I wipe my eyes and nose, embarrassed. There is one thing she can do, but I don't know if she will.

"Tell me why the music program was cut," I say. "Why are they getting rid of music, and keeping all the subjects I hate?"

Ms. Rinalli sighs, as if she knew this was the reason I was crying all along. "It's just money, Sam. Everything costs money, and there's not enough to fund the music program next year."

Money. I don't have a real drum set because there's no money. I can't take private lessons because there's no money. My parents are always stressed and angry and fighting with each other because there's no money. Why is everything *always* about money? Is there anything in this awful world other than money?

"What happens to you next year?" I ask.

"I find a job somewhere else," she says.

Find a job somewhere else. She says it like it's the simplest thing in the world. My father had to find a job somewhere else. How well has that turned out for him?

I wipe my face with my sleeve and say, "Do I have to leave the music room right away?"

"I can buy you a couple of minutes to cool down," Ms. Rinalli says.

I put my face back in my hands. Ms. Rinalli exits her office. I hear her sorting music sheets outside, but I still feel left alone, which is what I need right now.

I wait a couple minutes for the tears on my face to dry. Then I walk out of her office and into the rehearsal room. Ms. Rinalli sees me and leads me out.

I head over to the sixth-grade wing and find Scott and Zeke roughhousing by their lockers. Zeke has Scott in a headlock while Scott is trying to lift Zeke off the ground.

"Will you two cut it out for once!" I shout. "I need to tell you something."

Zeke lets go of Scott's head and says, "Scott's busy telling me he's in love with Ms. Rinalli!"

Scott's face is red, an apparent side effect of smelling Zeke's armpit. "Shut up! You're in love with Ms. Rinalli's mom!"

"You're the one who can walk on his head while farting the word *hello!*"

"Both of you stop it!" I shout, and they look at me, scared and confused.

"Um, what did we do?" Scott asks nervously.

"Yeah, we didn't steal your marimba mallets, you know," Zeke says.

"I know you didn't," I say. "This is much more serious."

They look at each other, shrug, and look back at me.

"Music is getting cut next year," I say. I wait for this to sink in. I get another shrug from Zeke, and a dumbfounded look from Scott.

"That means band is over!" I say. "No symphonic band. No orchestra. Not even jazz band."

Scott's eyes open wide. He shakes his head. "Oh man, my sister is going to be mad!"

"Why are they getting rid of it?" Zeke asks. "Music classes never hurt anybody."

"Ms. Rinalli says it's all about money," I say.

Zeke and Scott look at me like my face is melting. Then Zeke says, "You found out from Ms. Rinalli?"

"Of course. Who else would know?"

I'm scared they're going to ask for more details, like how the conversation started and all the embarrassing crying that led to it. Thankfully, they don't.

"I guess I'll take applied arts next year," Zeke says.

"Applied arts?" I say, nearly shouting. "You think applied arts can replace music?"

Zeke holds up a hand as if to keep me from bulldozing him. "Settle down, Sam. It's not the end of the world."

"Yes, it is!"

I look at Scott, hoping for support, but he just shrugs and

says, "I'm with Zeke, Sam. I agree it stinks to lose band, but there are plenty of other classes. Maybe the three of us can get into another elective together."

My heart sinks. My blood boils. I would expect this from my dad, or my brother, or someone like Danny Lenix, who is better at being my own personal percussion instrument than playing the sax. But Scott and Zeke? I expected them to understand. I didn't think I'd need a headphone jack to make them understand something we have in common.

"How can you guys be like that?" I ask. "We don't get to have music class in seventh grade! Or eighth grade! No playing in bigger and better bands with cooler percussion parts! No playing on a full drum set!"

"Look, Sam," Zeke says, concerned all of a sudden. "I get how much you like music. You take things seriously."

"But Zeke and I aren't like you," Scott says. "Band class can be a lot of fun sometimes, but we don't really care if we're good."

"We took drums because most of the parts are one note played over and over again. You can have fun playing without getting too stressed out about messing something up."

The tears are coming back, but I push them down. I'm not letting another drummer see me cry. But that doesn't mean I can't be really, really angry at them.

"Are you guys serious?" I say. "You might as well not care at all! What did all that time we spent together in band mean? Was it all just an excuse to get out of class?"

The nervous way they look at each other tells me everything I need to know. They don't care. They never did, and they never will. They see drums as the *easy* instrument. But it's not easy. I've seen what good drummers can do. It's just that the material we play in band is, admittedly, really easy. Especially the percussion parts.

"So you guys don't think you know how to play," I say. "What about me? Do you think I know how to play?"

There's an uncomfortable silence. Finally, Scott speaks up. "Honestly?"

"Dude, don't. Just don't," Zeke says.

But he's too late. Scott already has the words locked and ready to go. "You're probably the worst one in the band."

Zeke sighs and throws his hands in the air while making a mock slapping motion at Scott. I kind of wish he really would slap him.

"Don't take that the wrong way," Scott continues. "You play some really fast patterns, and learn new parts quicker than anyone. But you're kind of sloppy, especially for symphonic band."

"Sloppy?" I say. "Like I'm playing on a garbage can?"

Scott's face turns several colors. "That's not what I meant! Your drumming is just messy sometimes." He hesitates before saying, "All the time, actually."

My eyes are burning. I'm blinking in disbelief, my eyelids banging together like two gongs.

"I didn't mean you were the worst drummer in the school," Scott says. "You could've been a leading player in beginning concert band."

But I don't belong in symphonic band. That's what he's really saying—I've been out of my league this entire school year.

"Sorry, Sam," Scott says. "I'm just being honest."

I want to say something back. Something really clever that will bite him right where it hurts. It's one thing to hear Danny tell me how terrible I am, but Scott is supposed to be my friend. Does he agree with Danny? Does he think I have no rhythm, and that I sound like I'm playing on a garbage can?

"Whatever" is all I manage to say.

CHAPTER 7

Maybe Scott is right. Maybe Danny and Johnny Parker are right. Maybe everybody is right.

Except me.

I could probably accept that and move on to other things. Normal things. I could try harder in math. Try making more friends. Maybe even break into my mom's makeup and smear it all over my face like Laura Wilson did when we were in third grade.

But it doesn't work that way. Not for me. I want it to. But I can't accept that music is over. I can't settle for applied arts like Scott and Zeke. I don't like anything else.

Turning a page in a book sounds like drums.

Mr. Warner writing algebraic equations on the board sounds like drums.

The sound of our feet slamming against the gym floor when we run laps sounds like drums.

When I'm so angry at Scott for hurting my feelings that my head starts to pound, I swear the pounding sounds like drums.

Even silence sounds like drums. They play in my head when I lie awake at night and listen to the hum of nothing.

Quitting drums is not an option. I have to figure out a way to keep playing, and teaching myself isn't good enough anymore. I need to reach higher. If there won't be any music classes next year, I'll need private lessons. And if I need private lessons, I need money. I can't get money from my parents, or my school, or anyone else. I can only get it myself.

I grab a sheet of paper and a pencil and bring it to my drum desk, shoving aside the encyclopedias and the Calvin and Hobbes snare drum. At the top of the paper, I write *Ways to Make Money*. Almost immediately, I know my title is incomplete. Private lessons are an ongoing expense. If Pete Taylor's lessons are thirty dollars for a half hour, it's a good bet most other teachers willing to have me as a pupil will ask for something similar. That means my goal should be thirty dollars a week, if not more. I look at the words *Ways to Make Money* and scribble below it, in big bold letters, EVERY WEEK. Then I underline it to remind myself how important it is.

What are things that need to be done every week? My chores, of course, but I rarely get my allowance since my dad lost his job, and it wasn't much anyway. Even if it was a ton of money, I can't rely on something so inconsistent.

So what kinds of things do other people need? Neighbors, friends, or relatives? I think back to winter when I spent the day after a big snowstorm shoveling snow. I made about twenty dollars that day—not quite enough, but a good start. It's been a warm start to spring, though, so snow shoveling is out of the question at this point.

Brian barges into my room with tape on his face, toilet paper wrapped around his torso, and a baseball glove on one hand, and says, "What are you doing?"

"I should ask the same," I say.

"I'm trying to start the first mummy baseball league. What are you doing?"

"Nothing you need to know about." I sigh and turn my attention back to my sheet of paper. Brian creeps up behind me, boosts himself up so he can be tall enough to look over my shoulder, and says, yet again, "What are you doing?"

I cover the title at the top of the paper with my hand. "Why do you keep asking?"

"Because you keep not telling."

"And I'm not going to, no matter how many times you ask."

My brother scratches his head. "What if I start singing Beethoven?"

"You don't even know who Beethoven was."

"I'll find out who he was and sing his songs at the top of my lungs."

"Beethoven is mostly instrumental, and the lyrics he did write weren't even in English. You can't sing his songs."

"I'll find a way."

He probably will. And it will be horrifying when he does. My brother isn't going anywhere until I talk, so I come up with an idea. "Tell you what, Brian. Let's make a deal."

He smiles innocently.

"I'll tell you what I'm doing if—and only if—you help me think of a way to do it," I say.

Brian nods and gives me a thumbs-up. "Yes! Just call me Idea Man!"

I shake my head and continue, "I need to make some money. Thirty dollars a week or more. You have any ideas?"

"What do you need it for?"

"Not so fast! You need to come up with a good idea first."

Brian pouts, but doesn't push it any further. He sits cross-legged on the floor of my room, puts his head in his hands, and makes a face like a baby trying to concentrate really hard on—well, you know what I mean.

Then he stands up quickly and says, "I've got nothing. What about you?"

I uncover the sheet of paper with the words *Ways to Make Money* <u>EVERY WEEK</u> at the top. Brian looks at it, makes an ugly face, and points at the center where I wrote *Shovel Snow* and crossed it out.

"There's no snow anymore," Brian says.

"No kidding," I say. "That's why it's crossed out."

"Okay, so what does a snow shoveler do in warm weather?"

"A snow shoveler doesn't do anything."

"No way! They *have* to do something."

"Yeah, they wait for the winter."

"That's all?"

I shrug.

Brian's eyes light up. "Lawn mowing! You could mow lawns!"

I ponder the idea. Brian does have a point. Lawn mowing

is a good idea. It's something I could easily do if Dad will let me use his mower.

That leads me to my next problem.

"Okay," I say. "Good thinking."

"Of course," he says. "I'm Idea Man, remember?"

"There's just one more thing you can help with."

Brian shakes his head. "No way. Pay up first."

"I'm not telling everything," I say. "I'll *show* you something that will give you a hint. Then I'll tell you more if you can help me with an idea again."

"Deal," he says. He tries to get me to pinky promise, but I swat his hand away.

I grab my drumsticks out from under my desk and show them to him. He laughs and says, "You eat with chopsticks?"

"Of course not!" I say. "They're drumsticks!"

He gives me a weird look, like I'm some sort of space alien. "You play the drums?"

I want to scream. Why is it so weird for me to play the drums? Or want to, at least. "You've never heard me playing on the encyclopedias?"

"Is that what that was? I thought you were trying to juggle or something."

"I hate juggling."

"Juggling hates you, too."

"Maybe it does. Anyway, that's all you get to know until you help me get Dad to let me borrow the lawn mower."

Brian's face tightens. His mouth droops into a frown. "Uh-uh. Dad will never let you."

"Come on, Brian!"

"Dad won't even let me have an extra glass of juice with dinner. Forget it."

Brian tries to leave, but I grab him by the shoulders and anchor him in place. "Please! You have to help me think of a way! If you do, I'll tell you everything."

"Nope. No way. I'm outta here!"

Brian leaves my room. My anger surges the moment he closes the door, and I throw my drumsticks across the room. They hit the wall with a smack and collapse to the floor, landing in the lap of an old stuffed tiger I've had since I was four. I can't seem to get rid of him.

Brian's right. Dad will never let me borrow the lawn mower. I can imagine a million ways the conversation will end, and none of them will be in my favor.

But I *have* to try. It's the only way.

During breakfast a few mornings later, I finally gather the courage to ask about the lawn mower. I've practiced reciting all sorts of reasons and excuses for why I need to borrow it. I even wrote a speech by hand and delivered my soliloquy to the mirror until I'd almost convinced myself to lend out the lawn mower.

It's just my dad and me in the kitchen when I finally go for it. My mom is upstairs somewhere, arguing with Brian about the shirt he wants to wear. I don't even want to know which one they're talking about. My dad is pouring a cup of coffee when I say, "Could I ask a favor?"

His eyes perk open and glare at me. His pupils sag. He always looks like this if he's grouchy and tired. Not a good beginning to our conversation.

"I was wondering if I could borrow the lawn mower," I say. "Just a couple of days a week."

"What were you planning on doing with it?" he asks.

"Mowing lawns."

"Don't be a smart aleck, Sam."

A cold feeling passes through me. I'm screwing this up already. "Sorry. I just wanted to make a little extra money mowing lawns for some of our neighbors."

My dad breathes heavily. I'm not sure if that's a good or bad thing until he says, "All of our neighbors have their own lawn mowers."

"I know, but—" I try to say.

"And the money you make mowing lawns won't cover the cost of replacing it if it breaks from overuse."

"Dad, I'm not going to break the lawn mower."

"Like you *didn't* break the can opener."

My mouth drops open. "That can opener was almost as old as me!"

"And the television remote?"

I wince. Yes, I did an amazing job of spilling pasta gravy on the TV remote the day I'd begged him to let me eat dinner in the living room while I watched one of my favorite shows. It seeped into the buttons and soaked the insides so that the only button that worked was zero. But that was only one time. It could have happened to anybody.

If he could only plug into my headphone jack and hear how much I want this. Because no matter how hard I try, I can't put how important this is into a coherent sentence.

"Sam," my dad says, his voice calm, but not any less serious, "I'd love to let you use the lawn mower to make some extra money. It's good to learn responsibility by earning your own money. But what would we do if the lawn mower broke? Cut the grass with a butter knife?"

I really wish he hadn't included that last line. Like I really thought that's what we'd do.

"Honestly, Sam, you should spend more time helping out

around here," my dad says. "How can you expect to do a good job for others if you can't do a good job for yourself?"

And it's those last words that tell me I have really lost this one. My dad is not going to give in, no matter how much I push.

I run downstairs into our dusty basement and through the door to the laundry room. Next to the dryer, shoved into a corner between some pipes and the laundry table, is the lawn mower. It's a small one, but I know how to use it. I even know how to position it so that it gets all the tight corners next to fences and gardens. All I need to make this happen is permission, and permission isn't going to come.

There's only one way I'm getting this lawn mower.

It's not a good way. It's a really bad way, to be honest. Risky, too. I can't believe I'm even thinking it. If I hadn't overheard Ms. Rinalli talking about music being cut next year, I wouldn't have even considered it. But I'm desperate. I need to do what's necessary.

Brian has Little League baseball games every Saturday, and my mom will be gone with him all day. My dad's new job makes him work Saturdays. My parents won't even know it's gone. If I can't get permission to use the lawn mower, I'll just have to use it without permission. It's the only way.

CHAPTER 8

I know I'm being dishonest. But it's not like I'm Scott or Zeke. Or Johnny Parker, already performing like the perfect rock star he thinks he is. I can't stop caring on command. I can't snap my fingers and magically make my parents rich. I'm working hard to accomplish and earn something, and if I have to lie to my dad a little along the way, that's forgivable, right?

I'm thinking the hard part's already over. I've got a lawn mower—now I just have to find some customers. Lawns aren't all that big in Eastmont—property lines are pretty narrow this close to Chicago. Even so, three or four customers who are willing to pay me about ten dollars to mow their lawns shouldn't be too hard to find.

I set out on Saturday, midmorning, my planned day and time for mowing lawns. I need to know if this is going to work before I fully commit, so I leave the lawn mower at home, dedicating today to only finding customers. The first five people whose doorbells I ring all say they "need to save money in such a bad economy." Four of them say it nicely, but the fifth looks at me like I have potatoes falling out of my nose and says, "Ten dollars to mow the lawn? How about you pay me not to catapult you off my front porch!"

All I think to say in response is "You could have just said *no*."

I decide to venture out a few blocks farther from home, and I start to get lucky. I find one house that will pay me four dollars, and another that will pay me six. It's not great, but it's a start. That leaves me with twenty dollars to find. An old lady who lives next to a park says she'll pay me three, and even though that seems way too low, I agree anyway because she looks like she might be in her eighties and hasn't mowed her lawn in the last twenty years. I feel a little guilty I'm not doing it for free.

I start worrying it'll take way too many people to raise the money I need, but then I find a guy in a four-story house who offers me twelve dollars to mow his lawn. I thank him over and over again, jumping out of my skin with excitement.

I nab another customer, and I land squarely at thirty-one dollars. *Bingo*, I think. I've made my goal.

Wait. There's another problem: gas.

I need to replace any of the gas I use so my dad won't figure out what I'm doing. Gas is expensive, so I need one more customer to cover it. The only problem is I've blanketed the whole neighborhood. If I go any farther from home, I'll run out of time to finish all of my mowing before my dad gets home.

I decide to scope out houses I missed on my way back home. I figure there has got to be someone else who doesn't feel like pushing around a lawn mower every week.

It turns out I'm right. And the customer I find is the strangest one yet. I'm walking past Pete Taylor's house when I hear a raspy voice.

"You come around here a lot."

It's a hoarse voice, like its owner has swallowed sandpaper. I turn around and see an old woman standing on her porch. Her hair is a perfect sphere of curls.

"I guess I do," I say.

"What do you want with Pete Taylor?"

"Nothing."

She laughs. "You've been down this block five times today. You stare at his house like it's a chocolate cake every time you walk home from school. You'd better not be trampling my grass for nothing. All you kids going in and out of that house wouldn't be so bad if you would stay off my lawn."

Had I really walked past her house five times? I didn't think I'd been down this way even once today.

"I'm just trying to make money," I say.

"Money for what?" she asks.

"Does it matter?"

"It does if you're going to spend it on cigarettes."

I nearly burst out laughing. I expect to see her smile, but her face is as stern as a rock.

"It's for drum lessons!"

"Oh, so Pete agreed to take on another student?"

My head slumps. "Not really."

"Have you even asked him yet? Why don't you ask him?"

I already did over the phone, disguised as my mom, and he brushed me off like a dust bunny on his shirt. "Why would he give drum lessons to some random kid who showed up at his door?"

"Why give them to some kid who doesn't show up at all?" she says. "Listen, honey, if you don't have the backbone to knock on someone's door and ask an honest question, you're better off studying with someone else. Pete would eat a shy little girl like you alive anyway."

"I'm not shy," I say. But I'm still staring at the ground when I say it, so I bring my gaze back to her face and say it again. "I'm not shy at all. It's just—"

"You're afraid. Yeah, I get it. Have fun never trying anything new."

"It's not that! He's overbooked already. He already told me he's not taking on any new students."

She laughs. "He always says that."

"What does that mean?"

"It means exactly what I said. Just this week he took on another student from the high school. He's always overbooked, but I've known him for ten years, ever since he moved into that decrepit old house. I've never seen him turn away a new pupil." The woman's lips curl into a smile. "So long as the pupil proves they're dedicated."

That just confuses me even more. Why would Pete have told me he was overbooked if he's taking on new students? It doesn't seem fair. I called him about lessons before this kid from the high school. Why did he say no? And what does this woman mean about proving that I'm dedicated?

The woman turns for a second, ready to head back into her house, when she glances back and says, "How much do you still need?"

"How much what?" I ask.

"Money. How much more are you trying to raise?"

"Enough for gas for the mower."

"Then you can mow my lawn. Once a week, ten dollars each time."

My heart leaps. This woman must be joking. She must be part of an elaborate prank. There's no way she just offered me ten dollars to mow a lawn that looks like it was already cut ten minutes ago.

"You mean it?" I ask.

"No, I was talking to the squirrels," she says, annoyed. "Of course I mean it. Besides, you're going to need someone to buy gas. That stuff is dangerous. They're not going to sell it to a hoodlum like you."

I want to argue that I'm not a hoodlum, but hoodlum or not, most places won't like selling gasoline to a twelve-year-old. I'm probably going to need her help. "Thank you, but couldn't you get in trouble for this?"

"I'm eighty-three, honey. I'm not afraid of trouble, but this arrangement comes with an agreement from you." She points a single finger toward Pete Taylor's front door. "He's between lessons. You have a little less than twenty minutes. Grow a backbone, walk in there, and demand that he give you drum lessons."

CHAPTER 9

Ringing Pete Taylor's doorbell and asking—no, *demanding*—that he give me drum lessons should be easy, but it's by far the hardest thing I've done. My feet and calves are shaking. I always thought that was a joke, but being so scared that you shake is very, very real.

My index finger presses the doorbell, and the sound of its chime is like an electric shock through my body. Then it gets even worse. There's the sound of nothing, of waiting patiently. It goes on forever as I stare at the doorbell and wait for someone to answer the door. And as scared as I am to talk to Pete about drum lessons he isn't likely to give, I'm even more scared that he won't answer at all. Because I don't think

I can come back and try again. Not after knowing what this feels like.

Footsteps approach the door. Every ounce of blood in my body is ready to burst through my skin. The door opens, and a middle-aged man is standing there with the oddest look in the universe. He's bald on top with twisted strands of black and gray on the sides. He has thick glasses, a large nose, and way too much hair in his ears.

"Can I help you with something?" the man asks.

I try to talk, but my throat closes. I'm afraid a tidal wave of barf is all that will come out.

"Is something the matter?" he says, his eyes opening wider.

"I was looking for Pete," I say.

"That's me. What do you need?"

No way. This is not Pete Taylor. If it really is, he's totally not what I expected. I guess I was expecting something a little more, I don't know, rock starry? This guy looks like a crabby librarian.

"I need to ask you something," I say. "Could I come in and talk with you?"

"It's not the best idea to enter a stranger's house, young lady," Pete says.

"You're not a stranger. Everybody knows who you are."

Pete chuckles as he waves in the direction of the old lady's porch. She gives him a sarcastic smile as she waves back. "I doubt that, little miss. Either way, I'd prefer we keep our conversation on my porch. Now, what do you need?"

I swallow hard before asking. "I'd like to start drum lessons."

"Sorry, miss, but I'm overbooked as it is."

"No, you're not."

His eyes light up, and his face gets red. "Excuse me?"

"You took on a new student just this week. You have room for more students, and I want to be one of them."

Pete crosses his arms in front of him. "Let's say you were right, and I did take on a new student this week. Let's also say that even though it's true that I *am* extremely overbooked, I might consider taking on a student who shows promise anyway. What would *you* say to convince *me* that you're that student?"

I freeze. He has invited me to make my drumming speech. To give him my spiel, my sales pitch, or whatever I want to call it. Why should I be his student? I haven't prepped an answer, because I never had a plan—I'm only here because that old lady made me ring his doorbell.

Say something cool! Or smart! Think, Sam, think!

I have no idea what he wants to hear, but if my answer is wrong, I'll have wasted his time. I picture the only student of his that I know, Johnny Parker, and imagine what he would say in this situation.

"I've been in the middle school band for a whole year. I've played a variety of movements, know every percussion instrument inside and out, and can outplay anyone you're teaching right now."

"You can outplay that many people?" he says. "That's a pretty bold statement."

"And I'm going to be in jazz band next year. Or I *was* until they cut the program."

Pete's eyes look like they're about to pop out of his head. He clenches his teeth in anger and says, "Just when I thought I'd seen it all. I hadn't heard they were cutting the program."

I smile. "Nobody has, except me. I'm very informed, you know."

"That's fascinating." Pete looks at his watch and sighs. "Look, I have another student arriving in less than ten minutes. Thank you for stopping by, but you'll have to look for another teacher."

"What do you mean?"

"I mean this won't be a good fit. Try elsewhere."

"So you're not going to teach me?"

He shakes his head.

"Why not? I'm the best drummer in town!"

"Then you obviously don't need me telling you what to do. Go out and start your music career. You sound ready for it."

"But I'm not ready!"

Pete leans a shoulder against the side of the door frame. "Is that so? From the way you brag, you certainly are."

My fists clench and my toes curl. I want to storm into his house and start screaming. "That's not what I was saying!"

"Whatever. Look, I'm more than willing to take on another student. What I'm *not* willing to take on is another ego. I let a student go last week because he thought he was king of the hill, and the student who replaced him didn't show up at my doorstep acting like a busybody know-it-all. You picked the wrong teacher if you think that will work in your favor."

I stand there, my heart spinning in circles as the fire inside fizzles and drops into the pit of my stomach and explodes.

"Thanks, but no thanks," he says, and closes the door in my face.

I stare at Pete's front door, my energy extinguished. What did I do wrong? I'd tried to say what Johnny Parker might have said, and the reward I got was a door slammed in my face.

That's when I realize what Pete said: *I let a student go last week because he thought he was king of the hill.* Could it have been Johnny? Did I just screw up my one chance at getting what I've always wanted by trying to act like that jerk?

I knock on the door again. I don't even bother with the doorbell because you can't show anger by pushing something. When nobody answers, I check the door, find it unlocked, and walk in.

Pete is lying on the couch in his living room. The place is empty save for himself, the couch, and a practice pad perched on a stand next to a set of three congas. There is no television, no stereo, no anything.

"Is there a reason you've walked into my house uninvited?" he asks.

"When you slammed your door in my face, I heard a beat in my head," I say. "I imagined five different people behind five different doors of different sizes, slamming them in rhythm."

"That's"—Pete hesitates before continuing—"interesting."

"I hear drums in my head all the time. I can't even sleep most nights because it's like having an imaginary person in your brain who won't put their drumsticks down. It's amazing and horrible all at the same time. All I really want is a chance to make those beats happen somewhere outside my head, but I can't because I have no idea what I'm doing. I've tried over and over to teach myself, and my reward was finding out that I belong in beginning concert band."

"Says who?"

"Says the only two people I know who play drums. Only they don't even care about drums now that Eastmont's entire school district canceled its music program! So yeah, you're right—I was acting like I was better than everybody else. Everybody else seems to act that way, so I thought it was what you wanted."

I stop speaking, and there's silence between us for at least ten seconds. Pete blinks a few times and says, "Is that it?"

"Not even close, but I'm too embarrassed to keep speaking," I say. Wow. Where did *that* come from?

"What do you actually know about drums?" he says.

"That they're the greatest thing I've ever heard."

"You said you were in the middle school band. Which one?"

"Symphonic band," I say. "But like I said, I should probably be in beginning concert band."

"So what? It's still music class, isn't it?"

I smile. I hadn't thought of it that way.

"Is symphonic band the only time you ever play?" Pete asks.

"Yes, unless you count my desk set."

Pete gives me a weird look and says, "Please explain?"

I try my best to describe my desk set. I tell him what books I use, and what drum each book tries to replicate. He winces when I mention the Calvin and Hobbes snare drum.

"Wow," he says. "You need some serious guidance."

And even though it hurts to hear someone important definitively say that I have no clue what I'm doing, I say, "That's what I was trying to tell you."

"At least you have some idea how to set up a drum kit," he says.

"I've done it a thousand times in my head."

Pete leans forward and rests his arms in his lap. "But no one's ever really given you a chance."

"Less than that," I say. "Do you know how it feels to spend every day another step farther away from really learning how to play?"

Pete stands up and paces the room. I glance at him from behind and see that he's not totally bald. A long, black ponytail hangs from the tiny section of his head that actually has hair. It's the longest ponytail I've ever seen—longer than any of the girls' at school—and it hangs all the way down his back, dangling at the bottom of a button-down shirt that might look fancy if it was ironed and tucked in, which it's not.

"This is not a fad," Pete says. "This is not a hobby or a way to pass the time. Do you understand?"

"Yes," I say.

"I don't babysit. I teach young dreamers to become real drummers and real drummers to become really amazing drummers."

He used the word *dreamers*. It takes all my self-control not to bounce off the walls with happiness. "Yes."

"If I start to think you're wasting my time or not taking this seriously, you will be dismissed."

"Yes."

Pete crosses his arms and says, "That settles it, then. Do you have any other questions before you come back ready to work harder than you ever have before?"

I'm so excited that my voice squeaks a little when I say, "How much will it cost? Per lesson?"

"Fifteen dollars for a half hour."

I'm shocked. It must show on my face, because Pete says, "Is that going to be a problem?"

"No," I say. "Not at all, it's just, well—"

"Spit it out, missy."

I know I should just shut up and thank him. There's no need to bring up things he hasn't mentioned. But I'm curious, so I have to know. "I heard your regular rate was thirty dollars for a half hour."

"That is my regular rate. I'm charging you fifteen. Do you think you can mow enough lawns to make that?"

He knows about my plan to mow lawns. I never told him, but somehow he found out. I wonder how he knew, just long enough to realize I don't really care. He agreed to give me lessons. Mission accomplished. I feel a small tear leave my eye, and I blink furiously in hopes he doesn't notice.

"Any amount you earn over fifteen dollars goes toward saving for a real drum set," he says. "No more practicing on encyclopedias and comic books. Once you have a real set, we'll talk about charging you the regular rate. If I find out you're blowing the extra cash on video games, you're done here."

"Yes," I say.

"Three thirty on Monday afternoon is open right now. Can you make that work?"

I think quickly, sorting out times in my head. Mondays are one of my dad's latest work days. Sometimes he doesn't even make it home by dinner. My mom gets home around four thirty, so I'd have to rush home right after. I'd also have to leave school the second the bell rings, grabbing my stuff from home, and running to Pete's by three thirty. But it could work. It *will* work.

"Three thirty on Monday sounds great," I say.

"One of my biggest rules is don't be late."

"I won't. Thank you, sir."

"Another one of my rules is never call me sir. Or Mr. Taylor. I can't stand the sound of either. Just call me Pete, okay?"

"No problem, Pete."

"I'm serious when I say come prepared to work harder than you ever have before. I throw a lot of stuff at my newbies. A lot of them get spooked and don't show up for the second lesson. It would be disappointing if that was the case with you."

I nod and offer to shake Pete's hand. He backs away and says, "Get that thing away from me. Handshakes are for people who know they're ripping you off."

I consider this for a moment, and even though it sounds a tad silly, I don't offer my hand again.

"See you on Monday," he says. "Now get out of here and let me finish my day."

He returns to his couch as I walk out his front door and down his steps, butterflies flapping their wings in my chest.

I'm halfway down the block leading away from his house when it dawns on me what I've accomplished today. The tears shoot out, full force, like I'm suddenly the girly girl my mother always wanted.

I know I'm not a real drummer yet. But I feel like one for the first time in my life.

And it's all because I'm going to get a chance to learn how to play. *Really* play.

CHAPTER
10

I can barely sleep Sunday night. I keep envisioning my arms flying across toms as Pete cheers me on. Monday morning I feel like a zombie.

School isn't too bad, but my final lunch detention with Dr. Pullman comes at midday, and I'm not any less tired when he begins his interrogation.

"I still haven't heard from your parents," he says.

"They're really busy," I say, blinking my eyes to stay awake. "My dad works really late at his new job."

"I know. I tried contacting him at the office number we have on file and found out he no longer works there." He blinks several times, his gaze softening into something almost friendly. Scary Dr. Pullman is back within seconds. "Did you talk with them about contacting me, like I asked?"

My shoulders tighten. "I mentioned it to them. They're just really busy."

"Both of them?"

I shrug, wishing for a better excuse, but too tired to come up with one.

Dr. Pullman folds his hands in front of him. His eyebrows tense as he stares me down. "I'm concerned that you don't truly understand the severity of this. You hit another student with a *weapon*."

I shiver at the word *weapon*. Is that really what it was?

"I know it was wrong to hit Danny," I say, "but I wouldn't call it a—"

"I'm not concerned with what you would or wouldn't call it," Dr. Pullman says, interrupting. "You used the mallet as a weapon. You could have been suspended, but I decided to be nice and give you lunch detentions instead."

Suspended. Another word that scares me to death. My mallet didn't seem like a weapon at the time. It doesn't even seem like one now. It's just a wooden stick with a fabric tip that makes noise when it hits the wooden notes on a marimba. It's not dangerous. It's just music.

"I also find it more than a little odd that your parents are incapable of returning my phone call," Dr. Pullman continues.

I clamp my lips together as hard as I can, afraid that if I open my mouth, the truth will burst out. I focus instead on today's complimentary detention-based grammar assignments. I'm caught up on schoolwork now, but apparently there is an endless grammar vortex that I'm fighting my way through.

Dr. Pullman must be as tired as I am because he goes back to typing away at his computer. There's no more needling me with questions for the rest of the lunch detention.

The rest of the day is a blur. The moment the final bell rings at the end of band class, I sprint to my locker, shove my things in my bag, and run home. As tired as I am, the excitement of my first private lesson with Pete gives me a second wind.

I get to his house and ring his doorbell. When no one answers, I ring it a second time, growing increasingly nervous that he forgot.

He finally answers the door and says, "Give it a rest! If it's your lesson time, just come on in. You can wait in the living room if I'm finishing up with another student."

I follow him in, feeling silly and shy all at once. As he's

leading me down into his basement, a thought occurs to me. "I haven't mowed any lawns yet."

Pete turns around, giving me a look from the bottom of the stairs. "You do realize that's not what we're doing today?"

"I know," I say. "I just don't have any money to pay you. Not yet."

Pete chuckles. "Relax. If you still want drum lessons a half hour from now, you can start paying me next week. Are you ready to work hard?"

"I've never been more ready."

"Then let's stop talking about money and get started."

What I said is true. I *am* ready to work hard. Just not nearly as hard as Pete meant.

He begins the lesson by showing me his practice and teaching combination room. There are two drum sets—one looks nice and well-kept, and the other dented and chipped. Both look amazing to me.

"There are three rules. The first is never, ever touch my set. Students get to destroy that one," he says, pointing to the drum set with dents and chips. He gestures for me to sit by the student set while he sits by his own.

"How long have you had two drum sets?" I ask, jealous that I don't even have one.

"Ten years, give or take," he says. "Ever since I first started teaching. And before you ask—yes, the set in front of you has been in service that entire time. No, I don't know when I'll ever get around to replacing it. Probably never."

He grabs a pair of sticks out of a bag filled with millions of them hanging over the side of his floor tom. Then he does the coolest thing—he breaks into a heavy rock beat, and plays it with the most energy I've ever seen. Just when my brain is about to explode, he switches to a swingy jazz beat and breaks into a fill where he seems to play every piece of the set at once. He finishes it off with a crazy Latin beat.

Then he turns to me, and I can see that he didn't even break a sweat. He says, "The second rule is as simple as the first—the student who does not surpass her teacher has failed him."

I let his words digest in my head. Surpass my teacher? Does he really expect me to become a better drummer than him?

"That's impossible!" I say.

"With that attitude, it certainly is," he says. He grabs his ponytail in his hand and shows it to me. "There's gray hair in this nasty thing. You really want a guy with gray hair to beat you at drums?"

"But you've been playing for years!"

"And when you're my age, you'll have been playing for even longer. I didn't start playing until I was fifteen, so you've already got three years on me."

I try to imagine myself with years of practice under my belt. I imagine being able to do things on the drums I only dream about right now. I even dare to dream of myself playing the kinds of things Pete just played. It's easy to imagine, but I can't help feeling a little foolish at the same time.

Sam, you're such a dreamer.

"You said there were three rules," I say, trying to block out my mother's voice. "What's the third rule?"

"It's another simple one—the teacher doesn't have to know everything, just more than you do. It's a new rule, but an important one nevertheless."

Pete pulls another pair of drumsticks out of his gigantic bag and hands them to me. "It's your turn."

I stare at the drums in front of me and say, "What do you want me to play?"

"Anything. I just need to see what you can and can't do."

I try to think of something that will knock his socks off, but every beat I imagine feels cheap and childish. My limbs lock up. My shoulders clench. I'm freezing up.

"Any time now," Pete says.

"I'm sorry, Mr. Taylor," I say.

He makes a gagging sound. "Mr. Taylor makes me sick. My name is Pete."

"Sorry, Pete," I say. "I'm just nervous."

"No kidding. If you ever go on stage like that, you'll bomb the show for sure." Pete sits up straight and pushes out his chest. "Lucky for you, there's a cure for nervousness. One deep breath right before you start playing."

"Does that actually help?"

Pete nods. "One deep breath before you start playing, every time you go on stage. You may miss a few notes, but you'll never ruin your whole show."

It sounds easy the way he says it. I take a deep breath, feel the air entering my lungs and calming my body. Then I exhale, imagining a gray mist coming out of my mouth and nose. Then I play something. It's a sad attempt at a funky beat with the toms and snare, and I don't even work in the hi-hat. I've played something like it before at home, but playing it on a real set makes me realize how unrealistic my desk set really is. The positioning is totally different. Things are farther away. The stands can be adjusted, but I've never had to do that before, so I don't know how.

It also feels weird to play after him. All my flaws are so much more noticeable. It's so clear that he's really good and I'm not.

After about fifteen seconds of me looking like an idiot, he says, "Okay, I know where we need to start."

"I'm sorry," I say. "I know I'm terrible."

"That's ridiculous," Pete says. "You're undisciplined, not terrible. And for the record, being terrible at drums doesn't require an apology unless you're in the middle of a gig." He points at the sticks in my hands and says, "Forget all about the other drums for now. Just focus on the snare."

"I've played the snare a million times in the school band," I say.

"No, you've played it *wrong* a million times in the school band. Now you're going to play it right, and you're going to keep playing it right, no matter how many times your band teacher or your inept band friends try to tell you you're playing it wrong. Is that all right with you?"

I'm about to answer when I realize he was being sarcastic.

"Play me a single stroke roll," he says.

I freeze up. My arms won't move.

He lets out a big, long sigh and says, "Right left right left right left right left. Over and over again. Got it?"

"I know how to play a single stroke roll!" I say, not wanting to admit that I'm getting a little frustrated.

"Then what are you waiting for? Go for it!"

I take a deep breath, just like he suggested, and my arms

finally loosen. I start playing. Right left right left right left right left. He lets me play for about twenty seconds, and then he says, "Stop!"

I stop playing and look at him.

"Who are you angry at?" he asks.

"Nobody," I say, annoyed.

"That's a bunch of crap. You're mad at someone."

I'm mad at you right now, I think to myself.

He gestures to my hands. "You're holding that stick in a death grip, like you're wringing a chicken's neck. You're playing the drums like a homicidal maniac. Are you trying to kill your drumsticks?"

I shake my head.

"Then loosen it up."

I loosen my grip, and the rest of my body follows. He tells me not to slouch, that relaxing isn't the same as transforming into a hunchback, and then starts talking about my grip again.

"Hold it between your thumb and the first knuckle of your index finger.

"You're holding the stick too tight.

"Don't let the stick slip into your second knuckle.

"Don't squeeze with the other fingers. Just the thumb and index finger.

"Don't let the other fingers hang off either. You're not a flamingo trying to fly away.

"You're holding the stick in your second knuckle again.

"Don't clench your arms and shoulders. The only thing that should be moving is your wrists.

"It's slipping into your second knuckle again!

"Relax!

"Relax!

"Relax!"

And when I still don't relax, he says, "Pretend the cutest boy in school just threw a Skittle at your head."

My eyes bug out, and I say, "That wouldn't make me relax. That would make me want to punch him in the face."

"So punch him in the face if that helps. Then you can relax, knowing he got exactly what he deserved."

We both laugh.

We spend most of the lesson doing single stroke rolls on the snare drum. Whenever my arms start hurting, he tells me it's because I'm straining when I should be relaxing.

"Remember!" Pete shouts over my drumming. "You're not terrible, you're undisciplined!"

Then he makes me play double stroke rolls, which are even harder and more tiring.

Right right left left right right left left.

Back to single stroke rolls—right left right left right left right left.

Singles for four measures followed by doubles for four measures.

And on. And on. And on.

We do nothing else. I don't hit any cymbals or toms. I don't thump the bass drum. By the time it's over, I've been doing the same thing for what feels like hours, and it's only been thirty minutes. I feel like running out the door screaming.

While he's leading me out of his house, he says, "You're disappointed."

"No, I'm not," I lie.

"Yes, you are. Every student is disappointed the first lesson—you more so than most. It's okay. You won't hurt my feelings."

I shrug. Does he really expect me to have anything to say to that?

"You made it through your first lesson," he says. "How does it feel?"

It feels miserable and hopeless, but I'm not going to tell him that. Besides, the practice isn't what bugs me. It's something else. Something too familiar. Something I don't want to say out loud. That headphone jack in my head would be nice right now.

I take a deep breath and choose my words carefully. "I really appreciate what you're doing, Mr.—I mean, Pete. It's just that I've always hated the way they only let you play one drum at a time in band, and that's exactly what we did today."

"That's right," he says.

"I didn't think this would be just like band."

"It's not."

"Then when do I finally get to play the whole set?"

"After you learn to play a single drum correctly."

"Is that the only way?"

He nods. "Until you show me a way to juggle five beanbags without first learning to juggle two, I'm afraid so. You need to learn proper stick control and some drum rudiments that are actually useful. Then we'll see about moving you on to the rest of the set. Even then, Sam, I'm sorry to say that you will begin each session every week with stick control on a single drum."

"Oh" is all I think to say.

Pete walks to a corner of his living room and digs through a huge box of junk—mostly pieces of broken percussion instruments. He pulls out what I recognize to be a practice pad—a very small and very flat sort-of drum that tries, not always very well, to be a substitute for a real drum.

"Do you know what this is?" he asks. When I nod, he says, "Every practice session at home should begin with this. Single and double stroke rolls."

I take the practice pad and hold it in my hands. I stare into the flat rubber sort-of drum head and run my fingers along the circular metal edge on the side. "Does it have to be *every* time I practice?"

"Yes. I told you this would be hard work. The boring stuff is often the most important. If you want to get to the cool stuff, you have to stomach through the boring stuff so you can see how it all connects."

"Will I get to play the whole kit next time?"

Pete scratches his chin and shrugs. "We'll see."

My mom is still out when I come back from my lesson. Brian is in the living room watching a cartoon loudly enough to be heard on the moon. He used to have a babysitter, but that ended the day my dad lost his job. Now Brian walks home with a family friend and waits inside the house with the doors locked while my mom prays the house is still standing when she gets home.

When he sees me entering, he says, "Aw, man! Now the house will smell like farts."

"That's because you keep breathing on everything," I say.

I'm about to head upstairs when he says, "Dr. Pullman called!"

I freeze in my tracks. "Did he leave a message?"

"Yeah. He sounds mean. Isn't he the principal at your school? Are you home late because he kept you in detention?"

I ignore his questions. "Did you listen to it?"

Brian runs out of the living room and stops in front of me. He nods, a demonic smile forming on his face. "He wants to talk to Mom and Dad. You're in trouble again, aren't you?"

Chills run through my body. "If you say anything to them, I will wholeheartedly kill you."

He makes a gesture of zipping his lip closed and runs back into the living room to finish his ear-shattering cartoon.

I hurry to the phone, lift the receiver, and dial the four-digit code to access voice mail. It takes a little exploring to find, but before long, I hear Dr. Pullman saying,

Hello, Mr. and Mrs. Morris. This is Dr. Pullman from Kennedy Middle School calling again. I'm following up on a voice mail I left last week about an incident with Samantha. I understand you must be busy, but I'd like the chance to speak with you as soon as it is convenient.

I hear an undertone of anger in Dr. Pullman's voice. He's not going to let this go. He'll keep trying to reach them. And all I want to do is leave the message for my parents, let them know about the incident, and get the excuses and punishments over with.

But even though every part of my brain tells me not to, I press the 9 key and hear the words *"Your message has been deleted"* for the second time, and it feels even worse than the first.

CHAPTER
11

I wake up Tuesday morning, the day after my first drum lesson, with single and double stroke rolls sprinting through my head. I want nothing but time to practice. School, however, has other plans for me. I end up placing a notebook in my lap under my desk at the beginning of each period so nobody can see. Then I slide my hands on top of it and practice slapping out double stroke rolls with my palms. They haven't gotten any easier since that first lesson.

Right right left left right right left left.

I keep messing it up, over and over again, and halfway through math, I swear I'll never improve.

"Sam," Mr. Warner says, "it's hard to follow along when you don't have your slate out like everyone else."

I get my dry-erase board and marker out and halfheartedly try to solve the equations on the board. But my left hand keeps returning to the notebook in my lap and quietly tapping left left, left left, left left, creating half of the double stroke roll.

"Will you stop it, Sam!" Danny Lenix says.

I make a nasty face at him before stopping, but ten seconds later, my hand goes back to the notebook and starts playing again. It's like an automatic reaction.

I get a loud "Shhh!" from the girl next to me, and I stop again. Even Scott gives me this silent, scared look, like he's hoping I'll stop but is afraid I won't.

I glance across the room and see Kristen holding up her dry-erase board while Mr. Warner is looking in the other direction. There's a message on it in bold capital letters: TOO MUCH SUGAR?

I check to make sure Mr. Warner isn't looking my way and write NO. I HAVE RABIES. When I hold it up for Kristen to see, she clamps her hands over her mouth to keep from laughing out loud.

Danny sees us and says, "Jeez, you're annoying."

"Is there a problem, Danny?" Mr. Warner says.

I expect the bomb to drop right there, that Danny will rat out both me and Kristen. He must be intimidated by Mr.

Warner's angry glare, because he doesn't say anything, and the class goes back to normal.

It's not until the end of math that we start working independently on an extension of the lesson. I'm halfway through reading the directions when Mr. Warner calls me up to speak with him. I slide my notebook back into my desk and walk up to him. He lays a math test we took a couple of days ago in front of me and says, "I was curious what you thought of this."

I look at the test and the big, angry red D at the top. I'm not that surprised. I had expected a C and hoped for a B. Getting a D is pretty bad, though, even for me.

"I don't know," I say.

"Did you try your hardest?"

"Yes," I say, but the word *no* is repeating over and over in my head.

"Then what do you think happened?"

"Maybe I was distracted."

"By what? Something in class? Something at home?"

"All of the above."

Mr. Warner nods, like he's carefully considering his next words. "When a lot of things are bothering me, I focus on something I enjoy. What do you enjoy, Sam?"

An easy question. I wish every question in math was this

simple. "Well, I started drum lessons, and I want to work really hard at them."

"That's great! Are you enjoying them?"

I look at Mr. Warner and see real joy in his face. He's not just humoring me. He likes the idea of me playing drums. Everyone else thinks it's weird, but not Mr. Warner, who has never been on my side until now.

"I am," I say. "It's just really hard."

"Harder than math?" he asks.

I shrug. "In some ways, I guess."

"But you're working as hard as you can at drums, while you're not working as hard as you can in my class."

Aha, I think. That's where he's going with this. I should have known.

"It's nothing personal," I say. "Drums are *really* important to me."

"They should be." He puts my math test back in a pile of papers on his desk. "Let me ask you a question. What would you do if you had to play drums for your least favorite band?"

"What does that mean?" I ask.

"It means exactly what I said."

I think about it for a second. It's not a bad question, exactly. Just weird. But it does get me thinking. "I'd join another band."

"And if that's not an option?"

"Why isn't it an option?"

"Because another band wants to see how well you play before they let you join. They want to hire someone who's well-rounded. Someone who dedicates to a task when asked, knows more than the other twenty drummers in line to audition, and can play many different styles of music instead of just one."

"And I have to play with my least favorite band to prove that I know a lot?"

He nods.

"Then I'd rock my least favorite band senseless, and then tell them to get lost, and join the better band."

"Would you do your best for the crappy band?"

The word *crappy* throws me off. It's weird to hear a teacher say it. It's not really a bad word, but it kind of sounds like one, depending on where you say it and who you're talking to. It definitely sounds like a bad word coming out of Mr. Warner's mouth.

"Yeah, I'd do my best," I say.

"So if I ask you to do the same thing for math, then that would be a reasonable request, correct?"

As much as I hate to admit it, he has definitely backed me into a corner. "Yeah, that would be reasonable."

"All right, then. From this point on, you are free to get whatever grade you wish in math. The only thing I ask is that you try your best to rock math class senseless."

I shrug. "Don't take this the wrong way, Mr. Warner, but I don't think anyone can *rock* out in math."

"Then you need to go home and do a web search on *math rock*." Mr. Warner stands up. "The bell is about to ring. Enjoy the rest of your day, Sam."

Band has been awkward ever since Scott told me I was the worst percussionist in the band. Zeke still talks to both of us, but Scott and I only look at each other when Zeke is asking us both a question. I'm mad at Scott, and how am I supposed to talk to him when his comment sits like an elephant between us? It's not like Scott's apologizing, anyway.

Ms. Rinalli tells the band to prep the next song. Scott and I play dual snare drums, so we're forced to stand next to each other, an uncomfortable silence between us. We both pound through the song, our eyes glued to the sheet music. I catch Scott looking my way a few times, but his rhythm gets sloppy with each distraction, and he returns his attention to his sheet.

When the song is over, he looks at me and says, "You're holding the sticks differently."

I look down at my hands and then at his. He's gripping his sticks in the second knuckle. Pete would hate that. "I started private lessons," I say.

"Cool. It sounds better when you play that way."

I'm about to thank him when the bell rings, signaling the end of band and the school day. I put my sticks away and grab my bag. My hands fiddle through the front pocket of my bag and dig out a pen. I uncap it and write *Keep working on grip* on my left palm.

The students are filing out the door when I hear the tail end of a conversation behind me.

". . . plays on her notebook all day, and she's not even good."

I recognize Danny's voice right away, but I don't turn around. *Keep walking, Sam. He doesn't matter.*

"This whole band stinks," Danny says. "I can't believe I've been stuck in here all year. I know more than anybody in here."

"Yeah, I guess," the boy next to him says. Another sax player.

"I'm easily the best brass player here. Not that that's saying much."

Something about his last comment sets me off. I can take

him making fun of me—I've listened to that all year. Ripping on the entire band, however, is not cool. Not Ms. Rinalli's band. Not my band. Even if we *are* just a middle school band.

"You're not a brass player," I say.

Danny scoffs. "What did you say?"

"I said you're not a brass player."

"The drummer with no rhythm thinks she suddenly knows everything. What do you know about it, garbage-can girl?"

I reach for the pen I used to write the note on my palm. I so badly want to fling it at his forehead. My fingers clench around it, but I take a few deep breaths and calm myself. No more getting in trouble. Not for Danny. But that doesn't mean I can't put him in his place another way.

"More than you, apparently," I say, this time turning around and looking him in the eye.

"Saxophones are made of brass, loser!" he shouts. The volume of his voice causes the hallway to go quiet. Danny's forming a smile and an accompanying laugh meant to hurt my feelings. "That makes saxophones a brass instrument."

"Saxophones have a little something called a reed," I say, "and that reed is made of wood. That makes them wood-winds, but I guess you wouldn't know that, considering you're 'easily the best brass player here.'"

His smile disappears. He looks at his fellow sax player, who says, "Dude, she's kind of right."

Danny's face turns a few shades of red before he says, "Whatever. Have fun practicing on your garbage can tonight!" He storms down the hall. For once, he doesn't look back to make a mocking face.

Scott makes his way through the scattering students and taps me on the shoulder. "That was amazing!"

I smile back at him because that's what friends are supposed to do. I'm angry at him, but he's still my friend. It's funny, though. I don't feel amazing about getting the best of Danny for once. I just feel bad for him.

CHAPTER 12

I've been so focused on practicing for my second lesson with Pete that I almost forgot how I was planning to pay for them. But Saturday, the best day of the week, comes along, and my mom takes Brian to a Little League game and my dad goes to work, leaving me home alone with the lawn mower.

Kristen calls, asking me to hang out with her and a couple other girls, but I tell her I'm busy. I don't really want to hang out with people I don't know, anyway—not when there's so much work to be done.

The lawn mower is already full of gas, so I start my day fast. I mow lawns like a ninja. Time is against me, every second counts, and every lawn is a strategy waiting to be put into action. Should I cut it in this order? Can I save a minute or two cutting it this way? Perhaps I should mow the large backyard first, when my stamina is highest.

It feels good at first, but by the third house, I'm exhausted. One lawn is tough. A bunch of lawns is brutal. The sun becomes my mortal enemy, and I begin to hate it. I mock its placement in the sky and the way it casts heat down over the protective shadows of the trees. I start to hate noon and look forward to the later afternoon hours, when the sun will no longer beat down on me from the center of the sky. My baseball cap protects my face at first, but eventually it just makes my head hot, causing sweat to pour out the sides and onto my brow.

By the end of the third lawn, I am offered a glass of lemonade by the old woman who is only paying me three dollars. I tell her thank you and gulp down the entire glass in seconds.

"There really is no rush," she says. "I was going to suggest you take a break while you enjoyed it."

"No time," I say, gasping for breath. "I've got a full schedule."

She gives me a worried look as I move on to my next customer. By the time their lawn is done, I have given a new name to the sun. From this day forward, it will forever be known as the Orb of Death.

I imagine the Orb of Death laughing at me, an evil grin screaming down as I tire out with each trimmed row of grass. I invent a rhythm in my head and give it a melody—something about how I hope a bunch of asteroids take a big chomp out of its side. Yes, I know the Orb of Death is much larger than any asteroid will ever be, but that doesn't make it any less satisfying to imagine.

It takes a while, but I finally get to the last lawn. It's both the best and worst of the entire day. When I'm halfway through it, a woman from next door calls me over to the edge of the gate between the houses and asks if I'd like to mow her lawn as well.

And because I am either stupid or a glutton for punishment, I say yes.

I come home and leap into the shower. It's the best one I've ever had—I feel like I'm washing away a week's worth of body odor.

I get dressed in a comfy pair of shorts and a shirt. Then I collapse on my bed. The longer it is before I have to move, the better.

My skeletal system feels like it's falling apart, but I couldn't be happier. I feel in control. I am making a decision—a choice I can't possibly see myself regretting. For now, that's enough to make me feel good, even if my head hurts and aches and pains are throbbing through my arms and legs.

I lie on the couch until Brian and my mom get home. Brian runs down to the basement to do who knows what, and my mom sees me on the couch and says, "You look exhausted. What have you been doing all day?"

"Nothing." My arms tickle as the lies leave my mouth. "I hung out with Kristen."

"I haven't seen her around recently. I'm glad to hear you're still friends."

Mom leaves the room and goes about her late-afternoon routines. By the time Dad gets home from work, it's clear that no one has a clue what I've been up to. I breathe a sigh of relief, thankful that my routine is going to work.

Monday comes, along with a new rush of excitement. I hurry home from school the same as last week. I grab fifteen bucks out of a rolled-up sock in my top drawer, get my sticks, and run as fast as I can to Pete's.

He's waiting for me in his living room when I arrive. He looks at his watch and says, "Three thirty-two. I said don't be late."

"It's only two minutes," I say.

"This week it's only two minutes. Next week it will be

three minutes, and four minutes the week after that. I said don't be late, and I meant it. Do I make myself clear?"

I nod, apologize, and pull the fifteen dollars out of my pocket. He takes it from me, holds it between his fingers, and says, "You paid to be here today. Every minute counts."

We head down into the basement and begin our second lesson just like the first. Snare, and more snare.

We start out with a single stroke roll. Right left right left right left right left. He corrects me on the same things—keep the stick in the first knuckle, relax, only move your wrists.

He tells me to stop playing. Then he stands up, walks over to me, and points at three dents in the snare drum—three out of what looks like hundreds.

"You just made those," he says.

"Those dents?" I say.

He nods. I cower a little as my hair stands on edge. Did I just damage Pete's drum set?

"Calm down," he says. "I'm not pointing it out to get you in trouble. That's the point of this set. It's here to take any and all damage a beginner can dish out. I just want you to understand that we're not stabbing an enemy or blackjacking someone. We're playing the snare drum."

He sits back down by his set and tells me to continue. I

shake my arms, loosening the muscles, and try to imagine myself floating. When I start playing again, the snare hits are smoother and more even. Pete smiles and gives me a light, sarcastic applause. "Much better."

Then he throws me a curveball.

"I want you to play singles as slowly as you can," he says.

I do it. It's harder than you might think. The longer between each swing of the stick means the longer you have to screw up your grip. But I do get it down, and my grip feels better afterward.

"Now speed up just a little bit," he says.

I speed up.

"I didn't ask you to floor it, Sam! Take it easy!"

I slow down.

He watches for about five minutes, then says, "You got it. Speed it up again, *just a little bit this time!*"

I speed up. Then he tells me to speed up again. And again. Before long, I'm playing faster than I ever have before, but my arms are about to fall off. Little by little, the movement travels from my wrists to the rest of my arms and up to my shoulders.

"Are you tense?" he shouts over my lightning-fast singles.

"Yes!" I shout back.

"Slow it down until you're relaxed!"

I slow down. My body relaxes a little, but pain and numbness stay in my forearms.

I almost want to hug him when he finally says, "Stop!" My arms throb the second they stop moving, and the fatigue hits me, all the way through my shoulders and into my neck.

"I need to build up my upper-body strength," I say.

"No no no!" he says, waving his arms in the air. "You think drumming is all about power? Do I look like a bodybuilder to you?"

I'm not sure how to answer. Will I insult him if I tell him he looks like a pencil with arms and legs?

"Buddy Rich had the thinnest arms you'll ever see," he says.

"Who's Buddy Rich?" I ask.

His face turns red, like he just choked on a zucchini. For someone who's always telling me to relax, he sure looks like he's going to blow a gasket.

"You don't know Buddy Rich?" he says. "Why did you storm into my house, angry about jazz band getting canceled next year, if you've never heard a real jazz drummer play?"

"So he's a jazz drummer?" I ask.

"He *was* a jazz drummer. *The* jazz drummer. He had tiny

little arms like toothpicks because he never used his muscles, or lack thereof, to play fast."

"Can I borrow some of his music or something?"

"Do your parents have a record player?"

Whoa. Talk about old school. "Definitely not."

"Then you won't be able to listen to my collection. Head over to the library."

"The school library?"

"God, no! The public library. You can check out Buddy Rich's music on CD there. Totally free, as long as you bring them back on time. You do know what CDs are?"

"I'm not that dumb."

"You're not dumb at all. You're just young. That's why I don't want you going online. No torrenting. You're not going to get me in trouble with your parents, or anyone else, and most of his stuff is mislabeled by Internet idiots anyway. Torrenting Buddy Rich will probably get you Tina Turner."

"Who's Tina Turner?"

He shakes his head. "Just forget it. Your homework before next lesson is to listen to two real jazz albums. One can be Buddy Rich, and the other can be whatever you want, as long as it's jazz."

"Who else would you recommend?" I ask. "Besides Buddy Rich?"

"I'd recommend you find someone on your own. You're not afraid of jazz, are you?"

I think of how much I wanted to be in jazz band next year and say, "Of course not."

"Good. Then head over to the library and find a jazz album that speaks to you. If you can play jazz, you can play anything. Trust me. And if, by some stroke of luck, you discover an artist you've never heard before, it's a win-win situation." Pete gestures to the stairs leading out of his basement. "I expect you to be two jazz albums older when you show up next Monday."

I walk up the basement stairs and leave Pete's house, thinking about how to make it to the library. Wondering how I'm going to explain a sudden taste in jazz to my parents. All the while, another part of me wonders if my parents will notice, or even care about, anything related to music.

I wonder if it would be worth being busted, just so my parents could learn what really matters to me.

Another voice mail from Dr. Pullman is waiting when I get home. This one scares me more than the others. I had assumed the end of my lunch detentions meant the end of his phone calls.

Another press of the number 9 on the keypad. Another computer voice telling me, *"Your message has been deleted."*

Only it wasn't my message. Even I know that.

CHAPTER 13

The next day, before math class, I ask Kristen to go to the library with me after school. She agrees, but I can tell by the way she sighs that she's not as into the idea as I am.

We meet at our lockers at the end of the day and head over. It's a good distance, but we get to talk a lot on the way. When we finally get there and are walking through the front entrance, she says, "Seriously, are we really going to hang out in the library after spending all day in school?"

"You didn't have to come with," I say, hoping it won't make her want to leave.

"I know. It's just weird to come here without having to research something. This place totally wigs me out."

"Would it help to know we're coming here to get music?"

"Depends on the music."

I don't say anything else. Something tells me jazz would not get her approval.

I find the computer with the card catalog and search for Buddy Rich. When my search returns a bunch of books on him, I find the advanced search options and tell the system I only want audio recordings. That gets me what I want—a whole list of albums. It turns out the guy recorded a ton of stuff. Most of them are at other libraries in the area and need to be special ordered, but I find three that are in our building. I write down their location on a scrap of paper and run off to find them.

"So what's the deal with this guy, anyway?" Kristen asks.

"Buddy Rich?" I say. "He's a jazz drummer."

"No, I mean Pete Taylor. How did you get him to give you lessons?"

I try to tell her a short version of what happened the day I knocked on his door, and a little bit about our lessons. She winces at certain parts, as if my stories about Pete are like getting punched in the stomach.

"He sounds mean," she says.

I don't know how to respond. I can't argue with her—he isn't the nicest guy in the world, but I don't think he's mean. He just expects a lot. A *whole* lot. Maybe that's exactly what will ensure that I never hear anybody tell me I'm the worst drummer in the band ever again.

"Are you sure this is what you want to do?" Kristen asks.

I nod. "I've never been more sure of anything."

"What about your parents? If they find out what you're doing, they're going to lose their minds."

"I've been in trouble plenty of times. I can handle it."

"This isn't like bringing home a bad report card, Sam. You're stealing your parents' lawn mower to take secret drum lessons, all while deleting voice mails from the principal. Do you have any idea how insane that is?"

"I know. I just want to learn enough to practice on my own. After that, they can ground me forever if they want."

"Not forever. You're still coming to my pool party." Kristen frowns and puts a hand on my shoulder. "I'm sorry they cut music next year."

I put my hand over hers and squeeze.

We leave the library with four CDs. Two Buddy Rich albums, something by Miles Davis, and some CD that looks like it's covered in sparkles. Kristen says a new friend of hers says it's pretty cool.

It's still a while before Kristen has to be home for dinner, so we head to my house to find Brian building a fort out of couch pillows. He sees the two of us and says, "Help! The house is being invaded by baboons!"

"Talk to me like that again, and I'll kick you across the room!" Kristen snaps. My brother's face turns white as he retreats into his assemblage of pillows.

We race upstairs and drag out an old CD player I inherited from my cousin. We plug it in, pop open the CD deck, and put in one of the Buddy Rich albums. Kristen lies on my bed, and I lie on my stomach, my face inches from the CD player's digital display. I pull my baseball cap off and lay it on the floor next to the player.

The music starts off quickly. Quiet, but intense. There's a lot of piano and a faint, light percussion. It sounds like a drumroll on the ride cymbal until I realize he's playing that fast with only one hand. Then the snare and toms kick in, and he plays something that sounds like musical chaos.

"That is such a cool drum fill," I say.

"What's a drum fill?" Kristen asks.

It's hard to explain without that headphone jack, but I try anyway. "You know how there's the main beat that repeats over and over, and every once in a while, the drummer plays something quick and fancy on top of it? That's a drum fill."

"Like a guitar solo?"

"Not that long. Drummers don't play full solos very often,

but they're amazing when they do." I consider telling her about John Bonham's solo in "Moby Dick," but chicken out when I remember that awkward conversation with my dad about how Bonham died.

"So it's like putting glitter on top of the beat?"

"More like frosting, but yeah."

It's nice talking to her about drums. She doesn't give me any weird looks, and for a moment, I actually feel like an expert.

I listen to more of the music. The drums are constant and intense and totally in your face. I look back at Kristen, who's twiddling a lock of hair between her fingers, bored as I've ever seen her.

There are solos by other instruments—a saxophone, a trumpet, and an upright bass from what I can tell. None of them are impressive. It's not until later in the song that Buddy Rich takes his drum solo, the longest solo of all, and everything in the song stops to wait for him. Only they're not waiting for him. They're left behind in the dust, thrown from the vehicle, and tossed and spun across the pavement, lassoed and destroyed like a cowboy's victim.

The drum solo ends, and the band plays one more verse and finishes on one huge note that sounds like a thousand people playing all at once. If I looked at myself in the mirror right now, I imagine my hair would be a mess, my face would be flushed red, and my eyes would be popping out of my head. I don't know if I like the melody just yet, but I am absolutely blown away by the drums.

I have a long way to go, much longer than I thought, but my long road is not impossible. I can become that good if I want it and I'm willing to work hard enough. Buddy Rich was once a young kid who couldn't play a double stroke roll to save his life. That's why Pete said that I have to surpass him or I have failed. The only way to start learning is to see those who have done it and realize it's possible.

I spy Kristen staring at me, giving me this intense look, like my face just lit on fire.

She says, "Man, you're really into this stuff, aren't you?"

I'm too nervous to tell the truth, so I say, "I don't know."

"It's okay. It's not my thing, but I'm not going to make fun of you or anything."

"I know. It's not that." I push my hair behind my ears. "It's like the inside of my head was recorded and played back for me. Maybe that sounds weird, but it's the only way to explain how it makes me feel."

"That's cool." Kristen swallows hard and turns away from me. "If I knew how much you liked drums, I might have backed you up a little more."

She and I both know what she means. Her silence when-ever anyone made fun of me. Backing out of the conversation when I was getting picked on. Failing to do all those things friends are supposed to do.

And then there's me, realizing how hard it can be to do the right thing, especially if nobody's there to knock you off your pedestal.

"It's okay," I say. "You're still my friend."

I spend the rest of the school week fidgeting through class and listening to jazz CDs on repeat at night.

When Friday arrives, Ms. Rinalli opens rehearsal with an announcement.

"It is time to both celebrate and panic," she says with a smile, "because our spring performance is exactly one week from today!"

A few kids gasp, while others roll their eyes, pretending not to care. Others are just excited we're closing in on the end of the year. Those of us excited about the performance stay very quiet.

We spend the entire period playing our songs, trying to get through the whole list without stopping, and failing the majority of the time.

We get to the song where Scott and I play snare. He watches me intently, more so than before. When the song is finished, he says, "How are you playing your triplets?"

I look at my fingers, wrapped around the sticks. It takes me a moment to figure out what he means. "You mean my triple stroke roll?"

"Yeah. Whatever you call it."

"It's not a big deal. Instead of alternating snare hits, I'm playing three rights followed by three lefts. It's a good way to practice stick control."

Scott sits down and gives it a try, tapping out a triple stroke roll on his knees. It doesn't sound bad for his first time.

"You're getting pretty serious about this," he says.

"I am," I say. And I think, *I've always been serious about this, Scott. You just never noticed.*

Saturday arrives with a vengeance. I'm certain the second round of lawn mowing will be easier than the first. I am very wrong.

The day begins with me forgetting to visit Pete's neighbor first. I travel all the way to another customer on the other side of town only to remember that I don't have enough gas. I head back toward Pete's neighbor's house to find her waiting on her front porch, a portable fuel container next to her.

"Late start today?" she asks.

I give a little growl, and she laughs as she helps me pour gas into the lawn mower.

"You're helping me out, and I'm helping you out," I say. "But I still don't even know your name."

"It's Wanda," she says. "Then again, geezers like me forget things. Maybe my name is really George." When I give her a look, she says, "Loosen up, honey. It was a joke."

It doesn't matter that I'm more prepared for the physical exhaustion when I start mowing Wanda's lawn, because I'm still dreading how long the entire day will last. Last week I didn't know what I was getting myself into. Now I know precisely how bad it will be, and I hate every moment leading up to it. I hate how long I'm out there, sweating under the Orb of Death.

But this time I know the Orb of Death is no match for me. I've done this once before, and I'll do it again, no matter how many lawns it takes.

The old lady who brought me lemonade last week has water this time around. I guess if I'm going to gulp something down, it might as well be water.

When I've finished the last lawn, I'm pretty convinced

I'll never do it again. There's no way I can handle this every week. Then I remember Scott asking about my triple stroke roll, and feeling like a real drummer for the first time in my life. One horrible day per week is worth drum lessons, even if I have to mow a million lawns to pay for them.

CHAPTER
14

"Buddy Rich and Miles Davis?" Pete says from his little spot on the throne of his drum set. "Not bad for your first choices. What did you think?"

And all I'm thinking is, *Headphone jack, headphone jack, headphone jack,* over and over again.

"That bad, huh?" Pete says. "Did it scare you into silence?"

"No," I say. "I liked it. I just—"

Pete twirls his finger, gesturing for me to go on.

"I need more time to get into some of the songs," I say, "but Buddy Rich's drumming rocks."

Pete smiles. "Good enough. Now play me a double stroke roll."

It's the first time we haven't started out with singles. He's going right for the throat. I play them for a couple of minutes, until he says, "Not bad. Did you practice every day this week?"

"Every day except Saturday," I say. "I had to mow all the lawns."

"It shows. Let's try paradiddles."

I think the name is a joke until I see he's not laughing. Paradiddles are not a monster from a Harry Potter book or a dance move from outer space. They're a bizarre rudiment that throws me off even more than doubles. Right left right right left right left left right left right right left right left left. My hands are flying, wondering what the purpose is until I hear the pattern emerge:

PA-RA-DID-DLE, PA-RA-DID-DLE.

Right left right right, left right left left.

My hands really start to fly, totally relaxed but on fire, beating the tar out of the snare drum without me even having to flex my muscles.

"Yes!" Pete shouts as I stop playing. "There is hope for you yet!"

I beam a little, hiding my face so he can't see me blushing.

"Now play the right hand on the floor tom while keeping your left on the snare!"

I get goose bumps. *Did he really mean that? Did he really just ask me to—*

"Play on another drum? Yes, I did. It's the moment you've been waiting for. We're moving on!"

I move on. I play paradiddles all around the drum set. It's hard, but it's fantastic hearing my sticks make sounds all over the room.

The last fifteen minutes of the lesson is the best thing that has ever happened to me. I play paradiddles and three stroke rolls and four and five stroke rolls. I even play something called paradiddle-diddles that I swear Pete made up, but he assures me he did not. Everything's moving so fast, and yet somehow it's not fast enough, because I want to eat up everything he teaches me.

And then it's over. The second it ends, I desperately want it to be next week.

"Your homework this week is to search the web for the words *amazing rock drummers*. Pick two of the names that come up in your search and check out their music from the library."

Wow. Just when I thought this day couldn't get any better, Pete officially gives me permission to rock out. I'm so excited that I almost forget to give him the fifteen dollars in my pocket. I've never been so glad to give away money before.

Our symphonic band performance arrives fast that Friday. Every band kid dresses in dark pants, white button-down oxford shirts, and blindingly bright red suspenders, the last of which I consider to be a cruel and unusual form of fashion torture. They do this so they can gather in the auditorium on a stage that is much too small to hold them all and play out of tune for their parents. Totally my kind of night.

Zeke is his usual silly self, but Scott acts strange. He's even quieter than he is outside of band, and his face is frozen in a frown. It's hard to be mad at him when he looks so miserable. I try to strike up a conversation, and for a few moments, we're talking like we used to, but then it dies down and we're back to being silent nondrummers in the back of the band.

My turns come to play during the concert, and I do my very best, remembering what Pete said about learning to play one drum before trying to play them all. It's actually kind of easy to play my parts when I think of it that way. It's all so effortless. I don't get nervous, because for the first time in my life I feel like I know what I'm doing. Scott and I on dual snare are especially great. I even catch him smiling for the first time that night.

We all gather in the lobby afterward and meet our parents. My mom is there with Brian, waiting for me.

"You totally played in the wrong key the whole time!" Brian says.

"I was playing snare, idiot," I say. "It doesn't have a *key*."

"Don't call your little brother an idiot," my mom says. I wait for her to say something about the concert—how well I did or how proud she is—but I get nothing. No surprise there.

We're about to leave when I see Scott and Zeke together, making their way toward me, beckoning me to come and talk to them. I head on over, and Scott says, "I'm really sorry, Sam."

"Sorry for what?" I say.

"Are you gonna make me say it?"

"I don't know what you're sorry about, so yeah."

Scott sighs, slumps his shoulders, and says, "About what I said the day you found out music was getting cut. About you being better off in beginning concert band."

He's trying to make me feel better, but it's hard for that to happen when he's just reminding me of what hurt my feelings in the first place.

"You're better than I gave you credit for," Scott says. "You've improved more than anyone else this year, and if they weren't killing off jazz band, you'd probably make it."

"It's all right," I say, even though the memory of what he said still hurts and I'm not really sure it is okay. "You don't need to flatter me."

"I'm not. You're the only drummer here who cares, and it shows."

All right, I admit it. That last line makes me really happy. Even more so because I didn't expect it.

Jessica sneaks up behind Scott and says, "Time to go, my little bro."

Scott says goodbye and starts to leave the lobby. Jessica waits behind long enough to say, "Nice job tonight, Sam."

"Thanks," I say. Before I can think to clamp my mouth shut, I add, "Did you tell Scott to say those things to me?"

She looks confused. "What things? Is he being a jerk to you? Because I can handle him if he is."

I smile. "Not at all. Not anymore."

I head back to my mom and brother to find them speaking with Ms. Rinalli. For some reason, the sight of them together makes me nervous.

"Sam's come a long way this year," Ms. Rinalli says.

"I suppose she has," my mom says, smiling.

Ms. Rinalli sees me approaching and says, "Hello, Sam. I was just telling your mother the sad news about the cuts to

music. I really hope you find a way to continue with drums."
I catch Ms. Rinalli giving my mom a few nods, likes she's trying to say something additional without actually saying it.

My mom doesn't say much in response. "I suppose we'll see."

Ms. Rinalli gives me a final congrats, and I head outside with my mom and brother. It's not until I'm sitting in the back seat of my car, watching store lights illuminating the night, that I realize why Scott changed his mind about my drumming.

Pete's lessons. I'm getting better. And people are already noticing.

I dread my mom checking the voice mail when we get home later. By this point, I've lost track of how many times Dr. Pullman has called, and I'm terrified of his recorded voice. But there's only a message for my mom from my aunt and something for my dad from someone I don't know, and nothing else.

Finally, I think. *Dr. Pullman has given up.* Even though I feel bad for every time I pushed the button to delete his messages, I'm thankful I wasn't caught. I'm in the clear. I'm not getting into any more trouble.

CHAPTER 15

I'm finally able to complete Pete's homework the following day, after I'm done picking up gas from Wanda, mowing lawns all over town, and fighting the Orb of Death. A web search of *amazing rock drummers* gets more results than I imagined. And for every result that claims one thing, there's another claiming the opposite. There's no real answer as to who the best rock drummer might be. Just some names worth checking out.

There are so many choices that I end up picking three—Neil Peart from Rush, Keith Moon from the Who, and Dave Grohl from Nirvana and, more recently, Foo Fighters. I check out music from each band at the library and listen to them at home. Keith Moon and Dave Grohl play really fast and powerfully, and I swear halfway through every song they're going to break their drums in half. I find one insane video where Keith Moon starts breaking his drums on purpose! It's absolute madness as he slams his bass drum into the ground and kicks his snare and toms across the stage. Neil Peart looks calm in comparison, but he still sounds like he's playing the entire kit at once. I'm convinced he has eight arms and the energy of a border collie herding sheep.

Neil Peart and Rush also have a few songs that fit into a genre Mr. Warner mentioned—*math rock*. Some websites call it "progressive," but the ideas are pretty similar. Take away the rules that rock must have four beats per measure and a steady backbeat, and you get songs in time signatures of seven, nine, or even crazier stuff like thirteen. Unlike a lot of rock, there's almost no trace of blues, and it has a weird jazzy quality to it. I listen to songs by June of 44, Don Caballero, King Crimson, and a bunch of bands whose names I can't pronounce. I swear I'm cross-eyed by the end. That's what Mr. Warner must have meant—some music requires mathematical thinking.

All of them are good. Really good. But it leaves me with a question I have to ask Pete at our next Monday lesson:

"How do they only use their wrists when they play so loud?"

Pete pulls out his phone and loads a video. "Check out Neil Peart playing a solo," he says, handing his phone to me. "Yes, he moves his arms all over when he plays rock beats—it's called showmanship—but when he plays the really fast stuff, he doesn't move his arms at all."

I watch the video and see that Pete's right. Neil Peart flings his arms all about, looking tough and cool, but when it comes to the fast stuff, it's all in the wrist.

It's weird. I've always been angry when I play the drums. I even saw it as an advantage. But the more I learn about them, the less angry I feel.

The next two lessons have a set pattern—the first five minutes we talk about new music I've checked out at the library. John Coltrane the saxophonist, Ella Fitzgerald the singer, and more. For the first time since the conversation with my dad, I bring up John Bonham's solo in "Moby Dick," and Pete doesn't say anything about how he died. He just smiles.

Then we spend ten minutes playing singles and doubles and paradiddles and all other sorts of craziness. He makes me hold one drumstick a little higher than the other, and then I bring them both down in one swoop, creating the two quick strikes of a perfect flam.

The rest of the lesson is a powerhouse of new drumbeats

and patterns, each one cooler and harder to play than the last.

Then, at the end of the second lesson, Pete says, "I need you to do one other thing for next week. You need to dress in something nicer."

I look down at my T-shirt and jeans. My hand goes to my hat, lifts it off my head, and holds it in front of me. "What's wrong with what I'm wearing?"

"Nothing, as far as I'm concerned, but you had to dress up for the middle school band performance, right?"

I nod.

"Wear whatever they forced you to wear for that, and let your parents know you might get home a little later than usual."

I cringe at the thought of wearing those clothes and having to stay out later. My parents will freak if I'm not there when they get home from work. I can't just tell them I'll be missing for a few hours and expect them to understand. "Why?"

Pete rubs his chin and exhales. "I don't want to say too much. You'll just end up bummed if it doesn't work out."

I arrive home with my head full of daydreams about what Pete has in store next week. I try to get my mind off it by going back online and searching something else. Something Pete didn't ask, but I'm thinking he'll like. I click in the browser's search box, enter the phrase "amazing *girl* rock drummers" and click the search button. I wasn't expecting much, so I'm shocked when I get over twelve million results full of top ten and top twenty and top even more lists full of girls who've done exactly what I want to do.

Karen Carpenter from the Carpenters started out on drums, and sang while keeping the rhythm for the band. I never knew the drummer could be the singer.

Moe Tucker from Velvet Underground, who only used mallets (Danny Lenix would love her) and played while standing up.

And there's more. Gina Schock, Meg White, Janet Weiss, Carla Azar—the list goes on and on and on.

I'm not alone after all.

CHAPTER 16

All I know leading up to the following week's lesson is it's going to be something different. That doesn't bother me as much as the *getting home late* part. If my parents get home before I do, I'll be in serious trouble.

I talk to Kristen right after math just in case. "I need to tell my parents I'm going over to your house for dinner tonight," I say. "If they call to check, I need you to answer and cover for me."

"Sure," Kristen says, "but why do I need to cover for you if you're coming over?"

"Because I'm not actually going to your house."

"Okay. Now I'm confused."

I try to explain my mysterious lesson with Pete, and how

I need to convince my parents I'm going somewhere else as cover.

"Sam, you really should just tell your parents about the drum lessons."

"If you actually believe that, you don't know my parents."

Kristen exhales a dramatic huff, then shrugs. "Fine. I'll cover for you, but call me the second you get back so I know you're in the clear. If you get busted, you'd better not bring me down with you!"

I thank Kristen and give her the biggest hug possible, promising to make it up to her somehow.

I show up to Pete's house for my lesson later that day and am greeted by his disgusted face.

"What?" I ask. "Did someone yak on my shirt?"

"I asked you to dress nice," he says. "Are those really the clothes you wore for your school concert?"

No, of course they aren't. They're my regular clothes—always some variation of a T-shirt and jeans. I remembered that he wanted me to dress nice, but I felt stupid while I was putting on the white button-down shirt, black dress pants, and blindingly bright red suspenders. Once was enough. Do they really have to look that dorky? And does Pete really have to make me wear them?

"Go home and get changed," he says.

"Come on!" I say. "Do I really have to?"

"Why not?"

I'm silent.

"I'm not taking you to a beauty contest," he says. "I'm taking you to the Kirkwood Music Academy. I'm trying to get you into the recital."

Recital. Now I feel like an even bigger dork. Is this worth the risk of getting both Kristen and myself in trouble? "Aren't recitals for piano players?"

"Recitals are for musicians," Pete says. "And yes, most of them are excruciatingly boring. That's where I come in."

"You run recitals?"

Pete grunts and rubs his hands together. "No, Kirkwood Music Academy does. It's true that most of the kids they host play classical pieces on piano, or cello, or something like that, but they have on rare occasions allowed me to enter a student who shows promise to play a drum solo."

"You want me to play a drum solo?"

He nods. "You've shown a lot of natural skill in such a short time for someone so young. I was hoping they would take you, but you're not going to get accepted looking like that."

"Accepted for what?"

Pete snorts as if I've asked the dumbest question ever. "Your school is cutting its music program, and I can only bring you so far without practical experience. You need other musicians to jam with."

I swallow hard. "You think I'm good enough?"

"You could be if you stopped whining so much about a lousy outfit."

My fists clench, but I take a breath and allow myself to calm down. "Can I change back as soon as this is over?"

Pete nods. "The only other time I'll make you wear it is at the recital, assuming we're lucky enough to be allowed in this late in the game."

"When will it be?"

"In about three weeks. It's on a Saturday, so it won't get in the way of school."

If I had water in my mouth, it'd be coming out of my nose right now. "Only three weeks? When was the deadline to get in?"

"A little less than three weeks, actually. And the deadline was last Saturday."

I laugh. "Oh, well, that makes perfect sense, then. How exactly are you going to get me in?"

Pete smiles. "I have a friend who might be able to help,

but you're going to have to prove yourself to her—convince her you're talented and hardworking and not just looking for a place to goof off."

We walk through his house, out his back door, and enter his yard. My nose tickles with the smell of fertilizer and mold, blending together somewhere inside the long blades of grass all over his lawn.

We trudge through his yard and into his garage, where a small yellow car is parked. Black numbers—it looks like Sharpie—are written on his rear side window.

"What are those?" I ask, pointing to the numbers.

"Oh, that," he says. "I parked in a lot where I wasn't supposed to, so my car got towed. I keep meaning to wash those off, but I can't seem to find the time."

I creep in the passenger-side door and find the seat covered in music sheets and coffee cups. Pete throws all of it in his back seat, where a large amount of the same stuff has already collected, and motions for me to sit.

I tell him my address, and he drives me back to my house, where he sends me inside to change. Brian isn't home from school, so I don't need a cover story for him. I stomp all the way up the stairs and into my bedroom, scowling as I change into my black pants, white button-down shirt, and blindingly bright red suspenders. Last are my black dress shoes—they're supposed to fit, but dress shoes are sized to choke the life out of your toes and ankles.

I return to Pete's car and jump in the passenger seat. He takes a quick look at my outfit and says, "That looks better. You'd make a great Tiny Tim."

I flash him a nasty face, but he just smiles as he puts the car in gear and starts driving.

I think about Kristen covering for me as I drive into the city with a person my parents have never met to get into a recital my parents don't know exists. The opportunity to learn drums has changed a lot of things about me. I'm more confident. More brave. I'm also a liar, and I was never the lying type of kid. Irresponsible, maybe, but not a liar.

Pete's passenger seat is tiny and uncomfortable, with countless college pamphlets at my feet. I pick a few of them up.

"Are you going back to school or something?" I ask.

"Once was quite enough, thank you," he says. "I'm always getting junk mail from music schools. I pass them on to promising high school students."

"Are there really colleges where almost every class is about music?"

He nods. "Of course. Why wouldn't there be?"

I scan through Pete's junk mail and find a pamphlet for

the Juilliard School in New York. "Can you actually make a living in music?"

Pete hesitates before answering. "It's a lot harder than it used to be, but I suppose I'm living proof that it's possible."

Juilliard's pamphlet is full of crazy stuff—pictures of musicians and dancers having the time of their lives. Pete notices and takes the pamphlet out of my hand.

"Don't get ahead of yourself," he says. "You have plenty of time to think about college."

"Is Juilliard a good school for music?" I ask.

"It's *the* good school for music. In the States, at least."

"Do you think I could get accepted there?"

Pete sighs and shakes his head. "I told you not to get ahead of yourself."

The rest of the ride is longer than I expected. We leave the town of Eastmont and head into the city, taking the Eisenhower Expressway into downtown Chicago before heading off in a new direction. The Kirkwood Music Academy is at the end of a really crowded street and is noticeable only by a faded black sign that looks like it's going to fall down any second. We park the car in what I hope is a legal space and make our way inside.

"Let me do the talking," he says. "If Ms. Stanky asks you any questions, keep your answers short and polite. This isn't the time to showcase your inner firecracker. Save that for the recital."

"Her name is Ms. Stanky?" I ask. "Seriously?"

Pete gives me the worst evil eye I've ever seen. "Don't you dare crack up in front of her! She's heard it plenty of times, and she's not interested in being laughed at by a twelve-year-old."

I slump my shoulders. "Okay! I won't say anything."

Our conversation has made me nervous, so I grab a stick of gum out of my pocket and pop it in my mouth. I follow Pete through a few empty hallways. There's no one here, except for a few people in offices and a faint smell of books left out in the rain. Almost everything is made of a dark wood and squeaks when touched.

My clothes are uncomfortable. They rub against me in weird ways, and my body feels like a prisoner inside them. The dress shoes are probably the worst. Every step on the hard wood floor hurts my heels.

"Is that gum?" Pete asks.

I nod.

"Spit it out," he says, then looks around at the old wood and lack of garbage cans and says, "No no no, swallow it."

"I'm *not* swallowing it," I say. "That's gross."

Pete grunts and runs his hands over his beard. "Okay,

just don't let her see you chewing. She once found chewed-up gum all over the instruments in her storage room. Gum has been a banned substance in here ever since."

"Fine," I say. "I won't chew it." I press the gum against the side of my bottom teeth, wedging it in. Then I open my mouth and stick out my tongue, showing Pete there's nothing there. He waves me away and continues on.

We walk up a set of stairs and enter a very small office. A woman with crazy curly hair and faded clothes sits at a desk, giving us a tired smile as we enter.

"Nice to see you, Pete," she says. "It's been a while."

"It has, Pam," he says. "Didn't feel like coming around after last time."

"Understandable. Nevertheless, it's good to see you. What brings you here today?"

Pete points to me. "This is Sam. She's my newest student."

Pam looks closely at me, squinting her eyes. "So Pete dragged you all the way down here, did he? How are you enjoying your lessons, Sam?"

"They're good," I say. "I like your office, Ms. Stanky."

Pete winces, then quickly looks us both over. Pam looks back at him—nothing in her gaze shows offense at me using her last name. She says, "She's polite. I like that."

Pete laughs and says, "I'm not so sure it came from me."

Pam cocks her head and looks at me again. "I assume you brought her here because she's good?"

"Yes, she still has plenty of work to do, but she's up and coming."

"And her attitude?"

"Decent for a twelve-year-old."

"What's wrong with being twelve?" I ask.

"Nothing, in most cases," Pam says. "In others, everything is wrong with being twelve. And it stays wrong at thirteen, and fourteen, and sometimes even at forty-seven, like me." She leans forward and taps the top of my hand. "Don't you dare tell anyone my real age."

"I won't," I say.

She laughs and turns back to Pete. "What do you expect me to do with her?"

Pete sits back in his chair and folds his arms against his chest. "Put her in the recital you're hosting three weeks from now."

Pam laughs. "I can't do that, Pete. There's no room."

"There's always room. I know how you work. You always have a few empty spots for complaining parents."

"Is that what you are now?"

"No. I'm much worse."

Pam exhales and opens a drawer in her desk. She pulls out a small notebook and flips open the pages, scanning through it. Then she closes it, holds it out in front of her, and says, "You haven't told me why. Why should I put her in the recital?"

"Because she's worth it," Pete says.

"That's up to me to decide. All you can do is dress her up and pray I don't spot her flaws at first glance. And you know I'll find them soon enough, just as quickly as I found those of that last little charmer you sent here."

"I don't teach Johnny anymore. You know that."

Johnny? Does he mean Johnny Parker? That means it's true that Pete kicked him off his roster.

"You're a good music teacher," she says. "I'll give you that. But I never had problems with respect until I started taking your students."

"That was only one student."

"Yes. One student with the foulest mouth I'd ever heard. Do you remember what he said to my violinists? Do you have any idea what I went through after they told their parents?"

Pete's fists tighten, and so do my own when I see his temper flaring up. "She's not Johnny! She's only twelve, and she'll be wiping the floor with him before she's thirteen!"

"Then come back when she's thirteen, and maybe I'll reconsider."

That makes my blood boil. Another person in my life who thinks I can't do anything, and she's a musician. She should know better.

Pete looks desperate as he says, "Her school is cutting its music program! She doesn't have anywhere else to go!"

Pam shakes her head. "You think that's only happening to her?"

It must be a nervous reaction. I don't even notice my tongue flicking at the gum wedged against my bottom teeth, detaching it and flinging it back onto my tongue. I'm chewing frantically, trying to wear down my anger before I explode at this woman with a few words Johnny probably wanted to use when he was standing right where I am now.

Pam shakes her head, disappointed. Then she glares at Pete and says, "You didn't even tell her my rule about gum? Come on, Pete. Are you even trying?"

Pete looks at the floor, motionless. If I couldn't see his chest rising and falling, I'd think he'd stopped breathing.

"Let's go, Sam," Pete says. "It was a mistake to come here."

Pete rises and walks out of Pam's office. He leaves the

door open for me to follow, but I don't move. I stay where I am, still as a board and meeting Pam's gaze. Her eyes never turn away from me. Something tells me she is very good at staring contests.

"You seem like a nice enough kid," she says, "and I'll bet you're pretty good. But I swore to my superiors that I'd never work with your teacher again, and I meant it. I'm sorry you're caught in the middle."

My first instinct is to defend Pete, but I suspect I have nothing to say that she hasn't already heard. And maybe part of me believes she's right—the almighty Pete Taylor isn't the greatest drum teacher in the world, like I've always believed. He has flaws just like everyone else. Like me.

When I don't leave, Pam's face softens, but her voice remains just as stern. "I really am sorry. I wish I could help, but I can't."

"I know," I say. "I just wanted to ask if I could borrow a napkin."

"Don't have any."

"How about a tissue?"

Pam reaches beside her desk and pulls a tissue out of a big red box of Kleenex and holds it out for me.

"Any way I can bother you for two?" I ask.

She grabs a second tissue and offers both. I take them from her, cup them in my hand, one on top of the other, and reach into my mouth to pull out the gum I've been hiding.

"Garbage?" I say.

Pam points to the corner behind the door where there's an empty metal wastebasket.

"I know Pete can be a real pain," I say, "but he's the only person in my life who doesn't make me feel stupid for wanting this."

My thumb presses into the tissue and smashes the gum into a tight ball.

"I'm glad I met you," I say. "You don't make me feel stupid for wanting this either."

I throw my gum in the garbage. It hits the bottom with a loud thud.

"Thank you for seeing us," I say, "and sorry about the gum."

I turn around and walk out of her office. Pete is waiting for me but not looking in my direction. I don't blame him. It stinks when a good idea ends up a total waste.

The walk outside feels longer than the walk in. Everything I see is something I'm going to miss out on. Open doors filled with instruments I will never play. Rehearsal spaces where I will never rehearse. Recital rooms where I will never perform. It doesn't make me sad, exactly; yesterday I didn't even know this place existed. But it doesn't make me feel great, either.

As if things weren't bad enough, I notice something out of the corner of my eye—a father and son entering the building, headed our way. The father wears a suit that shines under the dim light inside the building. The son wears a button-down shirt and wrinkled tie, and he holds a saxophone in his arms.

It's Danny Lenix. With his father.

Our eyes meet for a split second, and we both turn away as fast as possible. Good. I don't want to talk to him right now, especially in this unlikely and unlucky place to meet. Danny's father, on the other hand, must be the social type— he recognizes me right away, approaches Pete with an outstretched hand, and says, "Nice to finally meet you. I ran into your wife a few times last year when our children were in fifth grade together."

Pete sees Mr. Lenix's extended hand and reluctantly shakes it, but doesn't correct him.

"I suppose you've also spoken with the principal at Kennedy about our children not getting along?" Mr. Lenix says.

Half of Danny's face is hidden behind his father, ready to explode with embarrassment. I look at Pete and cringe as I try to read his expression. It's surprisingly emotionless as he says, "I'm actually Sam's drum teacher, but I'm sure her father knows all about the situation."

Mr. Lenix looks surprised. He wrinkles his lips like he's not sure how to react. "I suppose I'll save my lecture for him. Let's go, Daniel."

Danny and his father walk past us without saying goodbye. I wait for Danny to turn around and give me his typical last-minute sneer while his dad's not looking, but even he finds this moment too embarrassing to harass me.

Pete and I walk outside to pouring rain. We find his car where he parked it, thankfully. At least one thing didn't go wrong today.

He unlocks the passenger-side door and lets me in. He's walking around to the driver's side with rain pelting down on him when I imagine Danny performing in Kirkwood. Smug face with a saxophone shoved in his mouth, his father in the audience, clapping the whole time. Something breaks inside me, and I start to cry. Pete enters silently, allowing me a few minutes to let it all out. He pulls a tissue from his pocket and offers it to me, but it's covered in lint, and I don't want one anyway.

When I finally get myself under control, he says, "You want to tell me what that was all about?"

I take a deep breath and tell him everything. About the mallet incident, and about Dr. Pullman's phone calls, and about stealing the lawn mower every Saturday to pay for lessons. Pete is silent the whole way through.

When he senses I'm finished, he says, "I suspected something was up, but nothing like this. You need to tell your parents, Sam."

He's the second person to tell me that today. The second person who doesn't get it. "I can't."

"Yes, you can. You can't hide how much you love drums. If it's that important, you need to share it with your family."

I wish Pete knew what that actually meant. Did his family understand when he made music his life?

"Promise me you're going to tell them," he says. "I can't keep teaching you in secret."

I wipe the damp hair out of my face and nod in agreement. "Just give me some time to figure out how."

"Deal."

Pete is starting up his car when his cell phone rings, causing us both to jump. He takes one look at the display and gets out of the car, leaving his keys in the ignition. His back faces me as he speaks to whoever is on the other end. I try to listen while he talks for a good five minutes, but all I hear is muffled words spoken barely above a whisper. I hope his cell doesn't get too wet—we've had enough bad news for one day.

He hangs up and gets into the car, soaking wet all over, and sits without a word as we listen to his engine rumble. After thirty seconds of uncomfortable silence, he finally speaks.

"I don't know how you do it, kid," he says.

"Do what?" I ask.

"Everything I can't do. Talk to people like you don't want to punch them, mostly."

"I do want to punch people sometimes. I just prefer marimba mallets over my fists."

Pete laughs. "Well, you have an amazing poker face, then."

I look him in the face, and it's weird. I've never seen him like this. I've seen him angry. Stubborn. Most of the time directed at me. Now, for once, he actually seems happy.

"What's going on?" I say. "Is something wrong?"

"Nothing's wrong, kid," he says. "That was Her Royal Highness, Ms. Pam Stanky, on the phone. You're in the recital."

CHAPTER 17

The rain has stopped long before we're out of the city and back at Pete's house. Pete tells me to think about what sort of style I might like to try for the recital. I thank him for taking me to Kirkwood, and he says a million times not to thank him—the best way to show my appreciation is to practice. He even refuses his weekly fifteen dollars, arguing that he didn't really teach me anything today. I disagree.

Pete offers to drop me off, but I decide to walk home from his house. I'm supposed to be coming home from Kristen's. It would look pretty weird if my parents caught sight of Pete's car while I'm walking in the door.

I'm just arriving home when I hear the phone ringing. I dash through the front hall to pick it up. "Hello?"

"Sam?" It's Kristen.

Then another voice on the line says, "Sam can't come to the phone right now. She's too busy picking her nose." My brother, the little brat, must have grabbed the phone at the same time I did. "I can have her call you back once she's dug out all the—"

"Get off the phone!" I yell.

There's a high-pitched scream, then a click, and then silence.

"Um, Sam?" Kristen says.

"Yeah, I'm right here," I say. "And I haven't been picking my nose or anything."

"As long as you're wiping them on his pillow." We both laugh. "Everything okay?"

"Fine. You could have gotten us busted calling here."

"You were supposed to call me when you got back. It's, like, eight thirty. I was starting to get worried."

I check the clock on the wall. She's right. "Sorry. I just got in. Everything's fine. Did my parents call to check up on me?"

"Nope. All clear." Her voice goes quiet as she says, "I haven't heard from you about my pool party."

That's right. I'd almost forgotten. Dr. Pullman never contacted my parents, so I'm not officially grounded. I should be clear to go. "When is it again?"

"It's on Saturday, about three weeks from now."

"I'll be there," I say at first. Then my mouth drops open and the hairs on my neck stand up. "Wait, I can't."

Silence at first. Then she says, "Why not?"

"I have a—" *Careful with the way you say it, Sam.* "I have a drum thing going on."

"A drum thing?"

"Yeah, it's like a recital. Only way cooler. I mean, not as cool as your party, but—"

"It's no big deal. Whatever."

I hear her breath quickening through the phone. She says it's okay, but I can tell when she's mad, and she's mad right now. She wouldn't be if I had that headphone jack to make her understand it's nothing personal. "It *is* a big deal, Kristen! I totally want to come. It's just that this drum thing is a music academy. I went to meet the person in charge tonight. That's why I needed you to cover for me. It's really important."

"More important than my party. I get it."

"Wait, Kristen. Listen."

"It's okay, Sam. I'll just talk to you later." The line clicks, and the phone is silent. Kristen is gone. I let the phone drop to the ground with a clang, not bothering to hang it up.

My brother appears in the nearest doorway and says, "Back to picking your nose?"

I can't even bear to look at him, so I cradle my head in my forearms to cover my eyes.

"Why did Kristen call? Weren't you just at her house? All you guys do is talk all day long." When I still don't say anything, his voice becomes quieter. "Sam? Are you okay?"

"I'm fine," I say through my arms.

The phone starts bleating its familiar off-the-hook warning. "Do you want me to hang that up for you?"

"No. I'll do it."

"I was just kidding about the nose-picking thing, and I don't really care how long you talk on the phone."

I press my eyes harder into my arms and say, "I know. I just want to be left alone."

Brian stares at me a few more moments before I hear him walk away. I grab the phone from where it landed on the floor and hang it up. Then I think about Kristen, and everybody else who will be at her party, and I sink to the floor, wondering why the things that make me happy make everyone else so mad.

I am going to do a rock solo.

Those are the words repeating in my head when I wake up the next morning. Not that Kristen is angry or my little brother is annoying—I have transformed them both into something else. I am going to play full-on rock, and I do not care what the classical musicians think about it.

I practice it in my head while I sleep and on my notebook underneath my desk during class. Danny is acting differently this week. He hears me tapping loud and clear, but doesn't say any of his usual insults. Not a single "annoying" or "idiot." I almost miss it at this point, but not that much.

Saturday arrives with a brand-new level of heat. Summer is kicking in, but oddly enough, I don't mind as much as I thought. I'm a tougher girl than I was when all this started. I mow Wanda's lawn first, as usual, only this time she congratulates me on getting into the recital.

"You and Pete talk a lot, don't you?" I ask.

"Every week," she says. "Sometimes more if I see him out in his yard."

Every week, I think. A crazy thought occurs to me. I ask, "Are you one of his students?"

She must see the shocked look on my face, because she narrows her eyes and says, "Is that so odd? Just because I've met Shakespeare in person doesn't mean I can't play the drums. My arthritis may keep me from hitting as hard as you rock types, but I still get the job done."

I smile at the thought. Wanda, the eighty-three-year-old

drummer. I can totally imagine what her lessons must be like. Something about a crabby old lady playing drums is just what I need to stay positive today.

I'm surprised to find Pete excited at our Monday lesson when I tell him my plan to perform a rock solo. I expected him to push me toward jazz, but he's all about rocking the Kirkwood Music Academy.

"Just make it something memorable," he says.

I fully intend to.

We spend the entire lesson designing it. Pacing it. Starting it off with something that builds, expanding it into new sounds, and giving it a climax that makes the whole thing soar. It's harder to do this than it sounds, but we manage to put it together a piece at a time.

I'm playing through it for what feels like the twentieth time when I smack the floor tom hard enough to shake the room. One of the legs on the drum's side buckles, and the whole thing topples onto the cement basement floor.

I grit my teeth and sit up straight, holding my breath. I glance at Pete, afraid to see his cherry-tomato face scowling back at me, ready to kill me for breaking his drum that was kind of broken already. What I see instead is a look of disbelief as he says, "You might want to take it down a notch."

"Sorry," I whisper. Then I pick the drum off the floor and fiddle with the leg stand until it's back in place and able to support the drum. Kind of.

Then Pete says something that scares me. "You know there's no way you'll perfect this in time, right?"

I wait for the goose bumps to go away. "Thanks for believing in me," I say sarcastically.

"I do believe in you. I just want you to plan accordingly. You're not going to perfect this, and you'll drive yourself crazy trying." He leans in closer. "You just need to make it sound like you care."

"I do care."

"Of course you do. Try playing through it again, and this time try not to destroy my floor tom."

I play through it again and mess up seven times before stopping altogether. Pete's right. I can't make this perfect, but I can make it look like I care.

At the end of the lesson, Pete gives me a stern look—the same kind as my teachers at school. He says, "What about your parents? Have you talked to them?"

I stare at the floor. "Not yet."

"You're putting me in a difficult place. I don't like difficult places."

I scoot my drum throne so that I'm facing away from him. "I promise I'll do it this week."

My teeth clench, and my brain throbs trying to think of a way to explain everything to my parents. I want to believe Pete understands and trust that he's right about telling them, because the thought of confessing sits heavy in my stomach.

CHAPTER
18

My upcoming recital haunts me the rest of the week. I can't concentrate on anything else. Even in band, all I think about is telling someone. Scott or Zeke. I should let them know what a cool opportunity it is. Every time I come close to spilling the beans, though, I imagine them in applied arts next year, not missing band one bit.

I'm halfway through the week, at the end of school on Wednesday, when I make a last-minute stop at the music room before heading home for the day. Ms. Rinalli is in her office, writing notes all over her teaching materials. When she sees me, she puts down her pen and comes out of her office. "Do you need something, Sam?"

I look back at her, dumbfounded, not knowing what to say.

"Are you having a problem?" she asks.

"No," I say. "I just wanted to let you know that I've been taking lessons with Pete Taylor."

"Oh, I know Pete. He's a bit odd, but he knows how to teach. His lessons are really improving your technique." She takes a seat in one of the band chairs near the front of the room. "You know, Sam, you definitely would have qualified for wind ensemble next year. Probably jazz band as well."

"Too bad that's not going to happen."

Ms. Rinalli smiles. "It's not all terrible. You're finding other opportunities. Just don't quit, okay?"

"I won't."

Ms. Rinalli starts to walk back into her office. I open my mouth again and feel a sudden tinge of embarrassment. I shove my shame down into the pit of my stomach in order to get the words out. "I'm playing a recital at the Kirkwood Music Academy a week from Saturday!"

Ms. Rinalli turns around. "That's great news."

"It's only ten days away, and I haven't asked anybody to go. If you wanted to come, though, I would be really glad to see you there."

Ms. Rinalli closes her eyes and sighs. I'm sure the answer is going to be no when she says, "Haven't you asked your parents?"

"Maybe. I think. I don't know." I sway from side to side, trying to shake my nervousness. "It's kind of a long story."

"Just make sure your long story ends with you telling your parents. I'll try my best to make it, Sam."

I thank Ms. Rinalli and leave so she can finish up her day. As I'm walking out, I spot Scott and Jessica talking at the other end of the hall. Scott leaves as soon as he sees me, but Jessica runs over in my direction. She pulls a set of brand-new Vic Firth drumsticks out of her backpack and says, "Scott *doesn't* want me to tell you that he *didn't* hear about the recital from Kristen. He also definitely didn't buy these for you so you could have a fresh set for the performance."

I'm not sure what shocks me more—that Kristen and Scott talked, or that Scott went out of his way to buy me brand-new drumsticks. I accept them from Jessica and run my fingers over the perfectly carved wood. Not a single chip or dent. "I'm not sure what to say. Can you tell him thanks?"

"No, apparently, because that would mean I told you they were from him, which I was specifically asked not to do.

Don't worry—I'll thank him anyway. Enjoy them, Sam, and don't use them until the recital!"

Jessica leaves, and I hold each stick in my thumb and first knuckle of my index finger. The rest of my fingers curl around them as I wiggle them in my hands, drumming an imaginary beat in the air, and admiring their perfect weight and balance. I chuckle as I put them in my bag and make my way home.

Another Saturday of lawn mowing arrives, and with it another visit to Wanda in preparation for my battle against the Orb of Death. It's a week before my recital, and by now I hardly even notice the intensity of the work. I've built up stamina. Sure, it's tough and mind-numbingly dull, but compared to the first few times out, it's a cakewalk.

I'm halfway through the third lawn, ten minutes ahead of schedule, when I hear an awful sound. The mower starts sputtering, just a little at first, and then a lot, and the louder it gets, the harder it is to push. I can feel it catching the grass below and coming to a stop in front of me. When I try to push again, a patch of grass rips away from the soil. I push the big red button to prime the engine a few times and try to start it up again. No luck.

The sputtering sound usually means it's out of gas, but I remember filling it earlier today. A full tank gets me pretty far, especially with how fast I've gotten. Something else is wrong.

I start to panic. If the lawn mower is broken, I can't finish all the lawns I'm supposed to mow today. That means a lot of angry customers, no money for lessons, and, worst of all, a very angry Dad.

If he finds out.

You stole the lawn mower, and you broke it. Two lies. Two punishments. Two reasons your parents will kill you.

This is really not good.

I come up with a quick plan. I need to get home. There's that stash of money stuffed inside a sock in my top drawer. I've been saving for a drum set, but I have to use it to repair the lawn mower instead. It's going to hurt *so* bad, but it's what must be done.

I can also call some of my customers—I have most of their phone numbers—and let them know that I'll finish up in the next few days. But there are at least three customers, if not more, whose numbers I don't have. I curse myself for not asking for them. From now on, I'll get phone numbers and email addresses from everyone. The customers whose names I don't have I'll just have to visit on my way back from getting the lawn mower fixed.

Oh, man! Where can I get the lawn mower fixed?

I freak out. I don't know what to do, so I start pushing the lawn mower home, thinking I'll start there and solve my problem a piece at a time.

Man, I am so busted.

Only I'm not busted. Not yet. All I have to do is get the lawn mower home and take it one step at a time. My house is two blocks away. I'll get there if I just keep pushing.

Now I'm one block away.

A couple houses away.

I spot something that stops me in my tracks, every inch of blood inside me freezing as I see what's in front of my house.

My dad's car. He's home from work. But how? It's barely noon. He shouldn't be home for another five or six hours, unless he was—

Oh, no.

I turn around and start pushing the lawn mower in the opposite direction. If I can get around the block and into the alley, I can go through the backyard and into the house through the big door that leads to the basement. All without my dad seeing anything.

It's all working great until I come to the alley, which hasn't been repaired for at least two thousand years. Trying to push a lawn mower is hard enough, but getting it over cracks and potholes as tall as my little brother is almost impossible. I'm halfway to the gate leading into my backyard when I see a dent in one of the front wheels. I'm pushing too fast—the cracks and bumps are damaging the wheels. I've already broken it, and now I'm running it into the ground.

I get to our back gate and hold it open with my back while I pull the lawn mower through. I'm relieved once the wheels touch the soft grass—it's so much easier to push.

I run across the lawn with the lawn mower ahead of me and come to a dead stop at the solid, locked door to the basement.

Of course it's locked, I think. *Why wouldn't it be?*

I leave the lawn mower in front of the basement door and run to the kitchen entrance. I look through the window, checking for my dad. He's nowhere in sight.

All you have to do is open the door, run downstairs, open the basement door, and bring the lawn mower inside. It will be like nothing ever happened.

I throw open the door to the kitchen and poke my head inside. I'm just about to declare that the coast is clear when I hear:

"Sam?"

I turn to the left and see my dad reading the paper at our little breakfast bar around the corner.

"Are you okay?" he asks. "You look like you saw a ghost."

"I'm fine," I say, much too fast. "What are you doing home?"

"I do live here, you know."

"I know, but—"

"Sam, I'd rather not talk about it now."

I shut my mouth. I know when my dad means business, and this is one of those times. It also works to my advantage if he wants to be left alone right now.

I leave my dad at the counter and walk downstairs into the basement, shutting the door behind me. Brian is in the basement, doing whatever stupid things he does down here.

"Ahhh!" Brian says. "It's a real-life yeti!"

"Shut up!" I shout at him. He recoils at my voice, and glares at me like I've actually morphed into a giant snow monster. I can't say I blame him. That's exactly what I feel like right now. "Why are you even home?"

"My game was canceled. Mom dropped me off and headed to the store. Why are you shouting at me?"

I look at Brian's wide, frightened eyes. "Nothing! Just forget it!"

I head to the basement door leading into the yard. There are two separate locks on it. The deadbolt turns easily, but there's a metal latch that's always stubborn, and today is no exception. I yank at it, then push, then rock back and forth, and finally pull it out of its hinge and open the door. I run outside and grab the lawn mower, and then carefully nudge it down the four small steps leading into our basement and shut the door as quietly as I can.

"What are you doing, Sam?" a voice says.

I spin around and see my dad standing behind me, staring. The way he spoke didn't sound angry, but the way he's looking at me makes it clear that he is.

"Nothing," I say.

"What are you doing with the lawn mower?"

"Nothing." When I realize how idiotic that sounds, I add, "I thought I might mow the lawn to help out."

"The lawn is outside. Why are you bringing it inside?"

I have nothing to say in response. I just shrug and let out a pathetic grunt.

"What's wrong with the wheels?" he says, pointing at the bottom of the mower.

"I guess they got a little messed up," I say.

"And how, might I ask, did they get a little messed up?"

Chills. Everywhere. In every inch of me. My imaginary

headphone jack clamps silent like a cymbal caught in a closing fist.

The phone rings. I hear it in the background, followed by the light thumping of my brother's footsteps running to pick it up. A few seconds later, he appears at the door behind my father with a frightened look on his face. Does he know what's happening?

"It's for you, Dad," he says.

Dad looks at Brian, then back to me, and says, "To be continued." Once he's left the room, I lock eyes with Brian, who looks more like a scared three-year-old than a third-grader right now. He mouths the words *I'm sorry* and disappears again behind the door.

Sorry for what? The lawn mower? Why would he be sorry for that?

"Oh, hello, Dr. Pullman," my dad says. "What can I help you with?" It all comes together. Dr. Pullman didn't give up.

I don't want to move, but I don't want to listen to one side of my dad's conversation with the principal of my school either. So I walk out of the back room, past my father while he's on the phone, and place a single foot on the stairs leading out of here before my dad covers the phone's mouthpiece and says, "Don't you dare go anywhere."

I freeze.

"Uh-huh," my dad says. "She did what? I see. And the other student? Uh-huh. Yes. Well, yes, I understand. That is very serious. Yes, I take it very seriously. You tried to call how many times? Oh, my."

Even though I only hear the muffled rasp of Dr. Pullman's voice on the other end, I can imagine exactly what he's saying. And I can feel my dad's mood changing as he listens. My very angry dad.

My dad hangs up the phone and turns to me. His face is tense, hiding the rage I can feel behind it. His voice is almost a whisper when he says, "That was Dr. Pullman."

I stare at the floor.

"This is the sixth time he's called. He says he left five voice mails."

All I can hear is the *ticktock* of the battery-powered clock on the wall, its face a smiling cat. How can anything—even something that's not alive—be smiling right now?

"He says you hit another student with a drumstick," my dad says.

And even though I know it's the wrong thing to say, my stupid mouth opens nonetheless and says, "It was a marimba mallet."

"I don't care what it was!" he suddenly shouts. I jump at the sound of his voice.

"He told me my drumming sounds like—"

"Dr. Pullman says you were almost suspended! You're lucky you're still in school! We're lucky that kid's family didn't sue!"

I want to say something. Defend myself. Tell him how nasty Danny Lenix was that morning. How nasty he is every day. How half the school secretly wants to hit him with something. But nothing comes out, because even if I had a headphone jack, it would burst into flames the second my dad plugged in. Part of me even wonders if Dr. Pullman and my dad are right. Maybe it is a weapon, and maybe I am lucky to still be in school.

My dad's face unclenches. His voice is hoarse when he says, "Go to your room."

He doesn't have to tell me twice. I start climbing the stairs out of the basement, and am near the top when he says, "This conversation isn't over."

No, it definitely isn't. I don't think it will ever be over.

CHAPTER
19

My true punishment doesn't arrive until my mom gets home from the store.

She's the only one who enters my room the rest of the night. She says my dad is "too angry to look at me right now." She sits on my bed and makes me tell her about hitting Danny with the mallet, about the lawn mower, about drum lessons and wanting my own set.

"What were you thinking, Sam?" she says. "What would we do with a drum set?"

We wouldn't do anything with it, but I can't tell her that without getting in even more trouble.

"How would we pay for it?" she says. I want to show her the money sitting in my top drawer from all that extra lawn mowing, but that's the one bean I haven't spilled. And telling her won't help when she never hears what I'm trying to say anyway.

"Where would we put it?" she continues. "How would we control the noise? It would drive your father crazy."

"I would only play it during the day," I say. "When you're both at work. And I could keep it in my room. I've looked online and researched the dimensions and measured out a space where it would fit. It could totally work!"

My mom sighs and holds her fingers to her temples. "It's not that simple, Sam."

"I'd only play when Dad was at work! I swear!"

"Your father won't be at work anymore, sweetheart."

A broken cymbal crashes inside my heart. I'd suspected that was the reason he was home early today. Now it's official.

"He lost his job," I say. "Again."

"Don't say it like that," she says. "He didn't get himself fired. It wasn't a good fit from the moment he started there."

I say, "I'm sorry," like there's actually something I can do about it.

"It's easy to be sorry after the fact. I get that music is important to you, but you shouldn't be taking things that aren't yours. You shouldn't be erasing voice mails to keep yourself out of trouble. And your father shouldn't have to find out about these things the same day he loses his job."

I want to tell her I'm not the one who decided to call today, but I don't even know if that matters. She's right. I'm the one who lied. "I don't know why I did any of that stuff."

"You did it because you wanted something you can't have. That's not the way to get things in this world."

I look at her hands. Her wedding ring has been missing for so long the indentation on her ring finger is gone. My mom understands how it feels to want something she can't have. "I know," I say.

My mom stands up and straightens her clothes. Her makeup is a mess, especially the eyeliner running down her face. "Don't plan on leaving the house for anywhere but school. You're grounded until further notice."

She leaves my room, sighing as the door shuts behind her. I crawl to the end of my bed and hide my head under my pillow.

A few minutes later, I hear a soft knocking at my door. I don't answer. I don't feel like being lectured or yelled at again. There's another knock, followed by a slip of paper sliding underneath my door. I go to check what it is, and it's a sheet of printer paper trifolded up like a letter. It says so so so SORRY in big red letters next to an arrow pleading for me to open it.

I unfold the paper to what I instantly recognize as a stick-figure drawing of me inside. I'm wearing my baseball cap with dark lines of hair flowing out the sides, sitting behind a shiny red set of drums with sticks in my hands and a huge smile on my face. There are musical notes all over the page, flying across the picture like lightning bolts of sound.

Beneath the picture are the words *Love, Brian*. The O in *love* is the shape of a heart. Funny. I thought only girls did that.

I clench the picture to my heart and sob. For such a brat, my little brother can be really wonderful sometimes.

CHAPTER 20

"You didn't practice," Pete says.

It's true. I didn't practice. Not since getting busted two days ago, at least. Not even on my cheap encyclopedia drum set. I don't even know why I came to my lesson this week. If my parents find out I've left the house, I'll really be in for it. I'm under strict orders until further notice to go directly home after school and clean the house until my parents get home. I probably wouldn't have come if my dad hadn't gone out to run errands.

And I suppose I might have felt guilty about ditching.

"Don't just sit there," Pete says. "I want to hear you say it."

"Say what?" I say.

"That you didn't practice."

"I didn't practice."

"The recital is on Saturday."

"Yeah, it is."

"That's only five days away. Every minute counts."

"If you say so."

Pete narrows his eyes at me. "What's going on?"

"Nothing."

"No way. Don't pull this on me. Not after I made a fool of myself getting you into the Kirkwood performance."

"Maybe I don't want to be in the Kirkwood performance."

Pete throws his drumsticks to the floor. They clatter and roll all over the place, and the sound is so sharp I almost fall off my chair. I expect him to start yelling, but instead he speaks in the softest voice I've ever heard. "We're wasting our time, then."

"Okay," I say.

Pete stands up, his face red and tense. "So that's it? Your drive is gone? I put myself on the line, giving you lessons in secret, and now you're just giving up?"

No, that's not it. Or maybe it is. How would I know without that headphone jack to help me talk like a normal person? But I don't have a headphone jack, and I'm not a normal person. I can't say anything right, so all I say is "I don't know."

"That's not an answer."

"It's *my* answer."

Pete kicks over his floor tom. His stick bag flies off the side and spills onto the floor. The throne almost keels over. The whole thing startles me. This isn't Pete being angry. This is Pete in a full-blown meltdown.

"How can you pull this crap now?" he says. "You could be my star student within a couple of years."

"Maybe I'm not cut out to be your star student," I say.

"That's a lie and you know it! You're not like the others! You're not some rich kid who demanded drum lessons just to make Mommy and Daddy angry! You're the real deal! You paid for the lessons yourself, for God's sake! You know how many other students I have that pay for their own lessons?" He makes a big circle with his thumb and index finger and says, "*Zero!* You're the only one!"

"Well, I can't pay for them anymore! I promised you I'd tell my parents about everything, and I didn't! Now I've gone and broken the lawn mower and gotten busted for everything! I'm grounded, and I'm supposed to be at home dusting the house to earn back the money it'll cost to pay for the lawn mower I broke!"

Pete looks shocked. "Is that really what this is about?"

I shrug. What else am I supposed to say?

He sits back down on his drum throne. "Do you really think you're never going to play drums again because you broke a lawn mower?"

"It's not just that," I say. "I lied about a lot of stuff."

"You're twelve years old. Learn from your mistakes and be more responsible next time."

"It's not that easy."

"It's not?"

I turn away from him. I can't look at him, because as much trouble as I'm in at home, it does seem like a small thing when he says it that way.

"It's none of my business," Pete says, "but that's a silly reason to give up music."

"I don't have a choice," I say. "I can't even earn money to pay you, and I'm grounded until the end of time. All for that stupid lawn mower, and for hitting Danny with a marimba mallet and lying about it."

Pete laughs. "I've had students do a lot worse."

That gets me wondering, especially about Johnny Parker, who I'm betting didn't get in any trouble with his parents for what he said to Ms. Stanky's students.

"What would you tell my parents if you were in my shoes?"

"I don't know," Pete says. "Maybe there's nothing to say

right now that can make things right with them. But it makes me sad to see someone so young, with the heart of a lion, just up and quit like this."

Pete walks over to the student set where I'm sitting. He holds the ride cymbal, wincing as he runs his finger over the numerous dents that have destroyed its sound over time. "You know, I was planning to—" he starts, then stops.

"You were planning to what?" I ask.

He shakes his head. "Just forget it. I'm done with you."

I hide my face in my hands. "I'm sorry."

He waves me away defensively. "Whatever. It's your choice."

It *is* my choice. And because I can think of nothing but the look my dad will give me if he gets home before I do, I stand up and walk out of Pete's basement. For the last time. I don't say goodbye, and neither does he.

CHAPTER
21

The next day at lunch, Kristen finally starts talking to me again. I have no idea what to say to her. She doesn't seem so mad anymore, especially not after I tell her what happened.

"So there's no way you'll be at my party?" she says.

"No way," I say. "Even with the recital off, my dad will never let me."

"It'll be lame without you there."

"You don't get it, Kristen. My dad is seriously mad. More than *ever*."

I'm staring at my bologna sandwich, but I'm not the slightest bit hungry. I pick at the sides and drop peeled pieces of lunchmeat on my tray.

"You really deleted all those voice mails?"

"I thought Dr. Pullman would eventually give up."

Kristen grabs my hand and squeezes. "You can't be grounded forever."

I squeeze back. "I know, but it feels like I will be right now."

Another group of girls from a table at the other end of the lunchroom call out Kristen's name. She looks in their direction, and then back at me. We both know those girls will be at Kristen's party, and they don't much care whether or not I'm there as well.

"Seriously," Kristen whispers, "it's going to suck if you're not there." Then she looks back at the table of girls who are still calling her name and shouts, "I'm sitting with Sam today!"

I manage a halfhearted smile. We eat the rest of our lunch in silence. It's my fault. I'm not really a social butterfly lately.

After school on Wednesday, the doorbell rings. I don't answer the door. Instead I peek out of my bedroom, around the curve of the staircase leading to the front door, and see Kristen on my porch, talking to my mom. I don't hear anything they say, and that's probably for the best. I've already told Kristen there's nothing she can do to get me out of trouble.

Kristen hands my mother an envelope and leaves. An

invitation to her pool party, probably. I watch my mom as she runs her hands along the edges, maybe thinking about what she should do. A part of me hopes she feels terrible. Another part feels terrible for wanting that.

I guess I don't really know what I want right now.

Later on, I hear my parents arguing. Their voices get louder and louder until I finally hear my dad shout, "I don't care how many other girls will be at her pool party! Sam's not going!"

Well, then. I suppose that's that.

I get another visitor later in the day, closer to dinnertime. My dad answers the door this time.

It's Scott. Meek little Scott, who I've never seen outside of school until now. I want to run downstairs and thank him for the brand-new sticks, but the timing couldn't be worse.

My dad gives him the ugliest look I've ever seen, and I want to crawl out of my skin when I think about how horrible it is for Scott to meet my dad like this.

Scott takes out his wallet and pulls out a few bills.

"What's this?" my dad asks.

"My allowance," he says. "I was hoping it would help pay for the cost of the lawn mower." The money isn't even close to enough, but he's offering anyway.

"We're not a charity," my dad says, and slams the door in his face.

I run back into my room, dig my face into my pillow, and pray that no one else tries to help me. There's nothing anyone can do.

I rise from my bed and look at my desk set. I haven't touched it since I got busted. That was only four days ago, and there's already a thin layer of dust on Calvin's face. The *Tribune*s are already starting to show discoloration.

I grab my Calvin and Hobbes snare drum first. It wrinkles when I pick it up and stuff it into the tiny bookcase where it totally doesn't fit. Then I take each of my encyclopedia toms and stack them in the corner. I don't feel like asking my mom where they should go at the moment. I'm too upset to lift the heavy dictionary bass drum, so I shove it across the room with my foot until it's beside the encyclopedias. Last, I take the *Tribune*s and smash them up as small as I can and take them downstairs to the recycling bin.

I don't know why, but tossing away the newspapers, the cheapest piece of all, hurts the most. But it has to be done. I can't bear to stare at my rotting desk set anymore.

CHAPTER 22

I pull my lawn mowing money out of the top drawer of my dresser and count it. It's not enough for a drum set, but it's more than I thought.

I wish I could at least spend it on something useful. I could replace the lawn mower, but I only have enough for the cheap push-reel kind, and I doubt that would make my parents happy at this point—not after my dad's reaction to Scott offering up his allowance.

I put the money back in my dresser and wish for a way to fix everything.

I haven't spoken to my dad in days. I spend most of the afternoons after school and the nights in my room. Sometimes

I come down for dinner, a silent fifteen minutes of nobody talking except my mom. Every so often, Brian will make a face at me, and the two of us will laugh. It makes both of my parents angry.

My mom visits me in my room every once in a while. She asks me how I'm feeling and what I'm thinking of doing that night. I tell her "I'm fine" or "I don't know" every time.

"You shouldn't lie in bed all day," she says. "Walk around a little, or you'll waste away."

I wish she understood what part of me was wasting away.

"I don't want you to become lazy," she says.

"I'm not becoming lazy," I say.

She gives me a sad look. "No, I suppose you're not."

My mom and dad fight a lot. My dad brings up the missing wedding ring a few times because apparently that's fair game now. They say my name a lot. I lie in bed, and my hands tap out rhythms on my thighs as my parents shout on the floor below. Even with my desk set disassembled, I can't help practicing—it helps me stay calm.

It's the same exact routine until late afternoon on Thursday. My dad bursts into my room and says, "We need a few extra things for dinner tonight. You're coming to the store with me."

"Do I have to?" I say.

"Yes. Your mother won't be back for a while, and you're not sneaking out while I'm gone."

Where exactly would I want to go? I think.

I get up from my bed and follow my dad outside to the car, my mouth shut the entire time. He drives several blocks to the store and pulls into the parking lot as I desperately wish for this trip to be over.

We're getting out of the car when I spot a small yellow car with numbers written on the rear side window in black Sharpie.

My heart skips.

"Dad?" I say, my voice shaking. "Can I please wait in the car?"

"No," he says. "You're coming with me, and I don't want to hear about it."

We walk inside the store, and I see Pete at the checkout counter with the oddest possible assortment of groceries—steaks, a bag of bananas and avocados, boxes of Special K and Cocoa Puffs, and Liquid Plumr.

I look away a moment too late. Our eyes meet the second my dad turns around to tell me to stop dragging my feet, and then he's looking at Pete too.

My feet are suddenly stapled to the floor.

"Is that who I think it is?" my dad whispers. I try to nod, but my neck is frozen.

Pete grabs his bags and receipt and walks toward us. "I'm betting you're Mr. Morris?"

My dad frowns and says, "And you must be the drum teacher making money off my daughter."

Pete's eyebrows curl, but he manages a smile. "I think we need to clear the air."

"I should say so," my dad says.

The three of us exit the store. Pete puts his grocery bags in his car before walking over to us. He looks surprisingly calm. My dad does not. The parking lot is eerily silent.

"I understand that Sam has gotten herself into a lot of trouble," Pete says.

"Yes," my dad says. "For stealing and lying. I take these things very seriously."

"I couldn't agree more. I also agree with you for grounding her until further notice."

My dad laughs. "But what?"

Pete stops and raises his eyebrows. "I'm sorry?"

"But what? There's always a *but,* so get it out of the way so I can say *no* and be on my way. I have a family dinner to prepare, but I suppose you wouldn't understand that."

Pete's face tightens, but he takes a breath and settles. "It's just a suggestion, Mr. Morris, and I mean it with all due respect. Keep your punishments all the same, but allow Sam to continue with music."

"What does 'continue with music' mean, exactly?"

"Let her perform in the recital this Saturday. If she does well, and I expect she will, a lot of doors will open for her. If that ends up being the case, I would ask you to allow her to continue private lessons."

My dad scratches his chin. "There's only one problem."

Pete's eyebrows rise again. "And that is?"

"This whole thing—the lessons, the recital, whatever—it all started because Sam lied."

"I understand."

My dad clears his throat. "No, you obviously don't. Sam began lessons with you because she did things that were wrong. To continue lessons and recitals and whatever else you demand a week or a month from now encourages her to lie in the future."

"I have no intention of teaching Sam bad habits. I fully support your parental decisions. I just want Sam to continue studying music."

"Why? To fill your wallet?"

I meet eyes with Pete, who now can't seem to hide his offense.

My dad points at him and says, "How much were you charging my daughter, anyway? How much does fraud of a twelve-year-old pay nowadays? How long have you known that my daughter was lying to us so that the two of you could meet without our permission?"

Pete's jaw drops. "Mr. Morris, please rest assured that I encouraged Sam to tell you about our lessons the moment I realized you and your wife were out of the loop. As for what I charge, the price can be adjusted to suit your family's budget."

"Well, now you know, and as far as you're concerned, you'd like things to continue just as they had before."

"I just don't want her to give up music." Pete reaches with his hands like he's holding an invisible object out to my dad. "With all due respect, you've never heard her play. She's extremely dedicated. It's astounding what she was able to learn on her own, and with my help, she's grasping the material I throw at her better than some of my high school students. Think of what she'll be capable of when she's approaching college."

My dad shakes his head. "Let's say you're right, and my daughter is some kind of drum prodigy. How does that help us? You'll still find some way to charge outrageous prices, we'll still pay through the roof, all while my daughter learns that lying and stealing are okay if you really want something you can't have."

"There are ways around the money," Pete says. "It might not cost you anything in the end. There are high schools that give out full scholarships to kids who aren't anywhere near as good as Sam will be by her freshman year if she keeps this up."

"Oh, that sounds great!" my dad says. "So she gets to spend high school goofing off with burnouts, all so she can graduate with skills that are worth zero in the modern world! Great idea, Mr. Educator!"

Pete's face tightens with rage. This is the Pete I know— the one that sits across from me and tells me to stop whining and play another five stroke roll. "You think all musicians are burnouts who can't make a living? *I'm* one of those burnouts, and I'm doing just fine!"

"Pete, don't," I hear myself whisper. I want to stop him. Push him into his car or put a muzzle on his mouth to keep him and my father from killing each other. But there's no stopping him. I can see it in his face. He's set to explode.

"I'm happy!" Pete shouts. "Happier than anyone in your house! What are you contributing to the modern world, Mr.

Morris? A miserable kid who will never live up to her parents' wishes? How dare you do this to Sam! How dare you hold her back!"

I put my head in my hands. I'm sure this is not how Pete wanted their conversation to go, but I'm not sure what else he expected. I once wondered what would happen if Pete and my dad ever met. Now I don't have to imagine it.

Pete's face returns to its normal color.

"Get in the car, Sam," my dad says. He glares at Pete. "Don't ever talk to my daughter again."

I get into the passenger seat and stare at the floor mat as I hear Pete's footsteps echoing in the parking lot as he heads back to his car. The driver-side door opens, and my father gets in and starts the ignition. We drive home in silence.

My mom is back when we return from the store. She knows something is wrong when she sees we don't have groceries. "What happened? Didn't you go to the store?"

"Ask your daughter," my dad says.

Mom looks at me, so I exhale and say, "We ran into Pete."

"Is he your drum teacher?" my mom asks.

"Not anymore." I shrug and look at the floor. "He said I was pretty good. More than good, actually. I learn quicker than some of his high school students."

My mom almost replies, but closes her mouth and looks

away instead. I run upstairs to my room before my eyes burst with tears.

Brian is sitting on my bed when I enter, staring at my empty desk. He stands up when he notices me and asks, "Are you okay?"

I plop down on my bed. "We ran into my drum teacher at the store."

"Did he talk to dad? Is dad going to let you go to your recital?"

I shake my head as I curl my arms above my pillow and around my head. Brian must get the point, because he leaves right away, looking almost as bummed as I feel when the door closes behind him.

I must have fallen asleep, because I wake up with a start to the sound of raised voices downstairs. It's my mom and dad, fighting over something. I can't hear clearly enough to know what. It goes on for almost an hour before I hear my dad storm outside and drive away.

He doesn't come back for almost two hours. I hear him entering the house quietly, like he's tiptoeing. He goes into the living room and rustles around for about fifteen minutes, followed by a dead silence. He must have fallen asleep on the couch.

My mom enters my room shortly afterward. I pretend to be asleep. My eyes are shut tight, but I can both hear and feel her presence walking up to the side of my bed and kneeling down. An arm wraps around me and gives me a light hug that lasts longer than any hug I've ever gotten.

Then my mom whispers, "I'm sorry, Sam." I feel her embrace as I remember the sound of her voice fighting with my dad and know her wedding ring is not the only thing she has lost.

I want to say something back, but I'm not sure if I'm supposed to be asleep. Will I get in trouble for replying? Or will I get in trouble for not replying?

I don't have time to find out. My mom stands back up and walks out of my room. She closes the door quietly, leaving me alone in the darkness to wonder what I was supposed to do.

It takes even longer than normal for the drums in my head to quiet down and allow me to fall asleep.

CHAPTER
23

I've never cared less about a Friday before. The recital where I will not be performing is tomorrow, so I can't think of anything else. Friday is usually such an amazing day. The last day of the week, and the end of every period brings you one step closer to leaving for the weekend. But today doesn't feel that way. Going home doesn't feel much different from school. I'm always watched, accused, and judged in both places.

Mrs. Pitts is talking about the Great Depression in sixth-period social studies today. Money, more money, and how sometimes there's no money at all. Yeah, I definitely get that.

Another kid in class raises her hand and says, "Isn't it true that we're in a recession right now?"

Mrs. Pitts nods. "Yes, we are, and while it's not quite as severe as the Great Depression, it has been a very tough one."

My hand shoots up. Mrs. Pitts looks surprised to see it, so she calls on me right away. "I'm glad to see your hand up, Sam! Do you have something to share?"

"I get that there's a recession," I say. "And most people seem to say it happened because a lot of people made bad decisions."

A few heads turn to look at me. Eyes and ears focus on what I have to say. Scott sits up straighter than ever before, his eyes glued to me. Nobody's used to me raising my hand and speaking up in any of my classes, much less social studies. I don't talk about history. I just beat on things.

"Yes, that is generally considered to be the case," Mrs. Pitts says.

And since I still have everyone's attention, I continue. "And these bad decisions—or whatever you want to call them—who is responsible for them?"

Mrs. Pitts ponders this for a moment. "It's complicated, Sam. Opinions differ based on whom you ask. Some people might blame it on big banks, or on the government, or on lazy poor people or greedy rich people. At times it seems like they're blaming someone new every day."

My mouth trembles for a moment, and I almost lose my nerve. "Is it our fault, Mrs. Pitts?"

"Sam, I'm not sure what you mean by—"

"Would you ever blame kids for the recession? Are we the reason why some people have no money while others have disgusting amounts of it?"

Mrs. Pitts takes a deep breath. "No, Sam. Kids did not cause the recession."

I take a breath and get out the last part of what I have to say. What I *need* to say. "Then why are we the ones paying for it? Why are they taking away our parks and pools and teachers and jazz bands? Why, all of a sudden, doesn't anybody want to pay for that?"

Mrs. Pitts folds her arms against her chest. "That's an interesting question, Sam."

A few kids turn away. The ones who don't have peeled their eyes open to the size of cantaloupes. I'd be a little embarrassed if I still cared what any of them thought of me. Scott's eyes are larger than anyone else's. His look is an awful mix of sadness and hope. I can't help wondering what he spent his allowance on after my dad slammed the door in his face.

"I'm not trying to be rude," I say. "I just want someone to tell me how that's supposed to be fair."

Mrs. Pitts frowns. She looks to the floor, as if the answer to my question is hidden somewhere in the tiles. When she meets my gaze again, her eyes are tired and heavy.

"It's not fair, Sam," she says. "It's not fair at all."

After school I'm in my room again, my hands tapping on my thighs.

Right left right left right left right left right left.

Give it up, Sam. It's over.

Right right left left right right left left right right left left.

Your dream of being a drummer is gone, just like your mom's wedding ring.

Right left right right left right left left right left right right.

This is getting silly. You need to stop.

Silence. My hands are still. I clamp them shut in my lap.

See? Was that so hard?

RIGHT LEFT RIGHT LEFT RIGHT LEFT RIGHT LEFT RIGHT LEFT.

CHAPTER
25

I spend the rest of Friday afternoon in my bedroom, dreading my forthcoming weekend of staring at the wall and eating uncomfortable meals with my family.

My mom comes to my room. She opens the door with the same sadness she's been carrying for days. It seems to get worse with every passing hour.

She sits beside me on my bed and says, "The recital is tomorrow, isn't it?"

"It was," I say.

"You must be pretty upset." She looks over at my desk. "You put away all those books."

I nod. "No point in having them out if I'm not learning to play."

"So you really did use them to practice?"

"Yeah. I had a book or newspaper for each drum."

She smiles for the first time in days. "Did it work well?"

I don't know if it's because I'm talking about drums or because my mom sounds happy, but my voice brightens. "It wasn't the real thing, but it was good enough. It helped me feel like a real drummer."

She looks closely at me, but I don't return her gaze. It's still too uncomfortable.

"Do you understand why your dad made this decision?" she asks.

"Didn't you both make it?" I ask back.

She hesitates before answering. "Yes, I suppose we did."

I look over at my empty desk. "You and Dad don't need to fight over it, you know. What's done is done."

My mom looks shocked. "We're fighting about a lot more than that, Sam."

I don't respond. I can't pretend it's not a little my fault.

My mom says, "Your dad is out with a friend, and I need to go to the store. I should be back and have dinner ready in about an hour or so." Then she stands and walks out of my room, shutting the door behind her. I wonder if she actually has to go shopping or if she just needs to get away for a while.

I think of the way my mom smiled when I told her about my desk set.

I rise from my bed, walk over to my dresser, and open my top drawer. I take out the lawn-mowing money and close my eyes as tight as possible. I finally kiss the dream of owning my own drum set goodbye and decide to spend the money on something else.

I have at least an hour until my mom gets home from the store. That should be plenty of time.

I wait until Brian is in the basement and my mom has left, and I quietly sneak out the door. I'm risking getting into way more trouble leaving the house, but I have to believe my family will understand my reasons when they find out.

My destination is near the bridge over the Eisenhower Expressway, so it only takes twenty minutes to get what I need. When I arrive back home with a small white bag, my mom is still gone and Brian is still in the basement, unaware that I ever left. I open the bag and pull out a tiny box that I place on the kitchen counter where my mom puts her keys when she gets home. She'll be sure to see it.

I dash upstairs to my bedroom, shut the door, and wait.

My windows are open, so I hear my mom pulling up outside when she returns. Her keys are jingling as she exits the car and walks toward the house.

The front door opens and footsteps head inside. They walk into the kitchen, but instead of the familiar clang of keys hitting the counter I hear the dropping of grocery bags followed by nothing at all.

A very, very long nothing.

Footsteps run up the stairs, and my door swings open to my mom staring at me with a heartbroken expression. The tiny box is in her hand, flipped open to a small wedding band.

"Sam," she says, tears filling her eyes. "Did you buy this?"

I nod. "I went to Silverlight Jewelers while you were out."

I expect her to scold me for leaving the house while grounded, but instead she asks, "Why?"

"I wanted to help," I say. The ring is shining under the hallway light. I'd considered pretending it was the real one, but I didn't want to lie anymore.

Her eyes look at the box, and then back at me. "How did you pay for this?"

I tell her about the extra money from mowing lawns, and saving whatever was left after paying Pete. Her eyes fill with awe. "How many lawns did you mow each week?"

Her jaw drops as I tell her about Wanda, and the old lady who only paid three dollars, and my strategies for mowing each lawn as efficiently as possible. I catch myself smiling halfway through, and my mom smiles back.

"You did all that work just for drum lessons?" she says. "You were saving every extra dollar to buy your own set?"

"It wasn't *that* much," I say. "I only had enough for a cheap knock-off ring. I couldn't replace the real thing."

She sets the box on my dresser and sits next to me on the bed, taking my hands in hers. "It's just a ring, Sam. It's not important. But that money—" she shakes her head. "You had special plans for it."

"I wanted to help you and dad."

"We're not fighting because of a ring."

My hands shake. "I know that. You're fighting because of me."

She pulls me close, and I bury my face in her arms.

My shoulders quiver in her grip. "I just wanted to help," I say again.

"It's not your job to help us," she says. "It's our job to help you."

My mom sighs as we pull away from each other. Our eyes meet, and something happens while we're caught in midgaze. Her expression is a puzzle, and the last few pieces push into place. Her eyebrows soften, and her mouth becomes a half-crescent as it gently smiles. I know before she has spoken that something has changed.

She pushes the hair out of my face and says, "We're returning the ring and getting back the money you earned."

"Why?" I ask.

She stands up and grabs the tiny box off the dresser. "Because I'm calling Pete. You're going to the recital tomorrow."

CHAPTER 26

The second she says it, my blood begins to flow again. An adrenaline rush floods my heart. "What do you mean?"

"I mean exactly what I said. You're going to your recital. Are you still up for it?"

My legs are suddenly spastic. "Of course I'm up for it."

"Then why don't you get started practicing?"

My hands are moving up and down. I want to drum. I want to drum like never before. But it's too good to be true. She can't really be thinking of doing this. "Why are you letting me do it? Why now?"

My mom sighs. "Your father isn't a bad person, Sam. He's just very angry about a lot of things. Things that aren't fair, but happened to him all the same. When you lied about the lawn mower and the incident in school, it was a lot for him to handle." She turns to me and smiles. "But I didn't realize how much this meant to you, and I can't stand to watch the fire in you go out any longer."

My eyes well up. My retinas tighten, holding everything in. "Does he know you're doing this?"

"Let me worry about your father."

"But Mom, he's so mad."

"Your father has spent the majority of his adult life mad. Another few hours won't hurt him."

My fingers tremble, and my mom notices. "You don't understand how he was the day Dr. Pullman called," I say. "You weren't here."

My mom takes my hand in hers and says, "I can handle him. Trust me. You're performing tomorrow, and we're going to find a way to continue your drum lessons."

Pressure builds behind my eyes. It's the pressure of tears I'm afraid to let fall, because I'm in front of my mom and I've spent so long turning my feelings off around my parents.

"Do you really mean it?" I ask. "Is it really okay?"

"Yes."

"Can you call Pete for me?"

"Yes."

"Do I need to do anything to—"

"Sam, the clock is ticking. Start practicing."

"Okay," I say, and then tear across my room in search of my drumsticks. I find them underneath a pile of dirty clothes and hold them in my hand for the first time in days.

It's the best I've felt since getting into the recital in the first place.

The good thing about having drums on the brain is you're always practicing, even when your desk set is disassembled and strewn about your bedroom. Your hands are tapping out rhythms and rudiments, and your imagination is dreaming up new ways to make beautiful noise. It's not the same as real practice, but it's something.

It doesn't take long to put my desk set back together, but when I actually try to practice, everything feels weird. Real drums have a rebound effect when you hit them with a drumstick. It isn't there when you tap on your legs. Even on my desk set, I can feel the difference. My flams sound like a giraffe falling down and my double stroke roll sounds like a goblin kneading bread. Pete wasn't kidding. I really do need to start every practice session with stick control.

After an hour or so of going through the motions, I'm

sounding better. It's almost like I never gave up, because in my heart I never really did.

My dad is staying out late with a friend he hopes will help him network and find a new job, so I practice until the sun sets. I realize how tired I am and settle down for the night, hoping my mom knows the right way to explain things to my dad when he gets home.

The drums in my head are louder than ever, but tonight they don't keep me awake.

My eyes fly open the next morning, the day of the recital. I run downstairs, find my mom, and shout, "Have you talked to Pete?"

"Good morning, Sam," she says with a hint of sarcasm.

"Good morning, Mom. Have you called him?"

"Several times, but when I dial his number, it just keeps ringing."

I run to the phone and call Pete, getting the same result. A whole bunch of ringing and a voice mail message that I know he ignores. I try one more time, get no answer, and tell my mom I'm heading over there. She politely asks me to change out of my pajamas first, and as soon as I do, I spring out the front door and down to Pete's house.

I forget to ring Pete's bell and burst through his front

door. Then I run downstairs into his basement and find him working with another student. I forgot he gave lessons on Saturday.

I expect him to scream at me for barging into his house, but all he says is "I thought you were grounded."

"I am," I say. "Well, I'm technically only half grounded now."

"Great! I'm glad to hear this won't get me into more trouble with your father, then."

"This is serious!"

Pete laughs and points to his current student, who looks so embarrassed his face might explode. "So is this. Can I have five minutes, please?" The look he gives me makes it clear he's not asking permission.

I run back upstairs into Pete's living room. I sit on the couch and hear a high-pitched *meow* as a small black-and-white cat pokes its head out from under the cushions and hisses at me. I hiss back, and the cat runs away.

I didn't even know Pete had a cat.

Several minutes pass, and Pete comes upstairs with his deer-in-the-headlights-looking student and walks him out the door. Then he turns to me and folds his arms against his chest.

"Your cat hates me," I say.

"He hates me, too," Pete says. "You found him inside the couch?"

I nod.

"Don't ask me how he digs his way in there. And don't worry about him—he doesn't scratch." Pete grabs a folding chair from the corner of the room and opens it in the middle of the hardwood floor, taking a seat. "Why are you back?"

I explain the conversation with my mom. He nods at all the important parts and tosses his tongue around in his mouth like he's thinking really hard.

"Your dad is going to find out," he says. "He's going to be upset."

That's an understatement. "My mom said she'll take care of him."

"Oh, I'm sure I'll have to take care of it as well."

"Not the way my mom said it."

"But I will. Your dad is not my biggest fan, but he's still a good person, and he won't have the heart to blame this all on your mother. He'll find someone else to take it out on. That will be me."

I sit forward on the couch. "Does that mean you don't want me to do this?"

"Of course I want you to do this. I just need you to make some promises first." Pete stands up and grabs a sheet of paper and pencil from a small drawer next to his couch. Then he sits back down in his folding chair and begins to write. "You will never miss a lesson without twenty-four hours' notice, and when you do, it will be for a really good reason. You will never show up to a lesson the way you did last time. Without practicing. Without showing that you care. With nothing besides a bad attitude. You will not waste our time. You will *never*, under any circumstances, lie to your parents about our lessons together. I will not be an accomplice to your dishonesty."

I stand up and extend my hand. "Deal."

Pete slaps my hand away. "What did I tell you about handshakes?"

My face turns red. "Sorry."

Pete scribbles one last time on his paper and hands it to me along with the pencil. "Sign it."

I take the paper and pencil from him and read it:

Number one: No missing lessons.

Number two: No bad attitudes.

Number three: NO LYING.

Underneath the third line is a messy scribble I assume is Pete's signature. I sign my name much more legibly underneath his and hand the paper back. Pete takes it from me and says, "It's a promise now. No backing out."

"I know," I say. "So what should I do next?"

"Do you remember what we worked on for the recital?" When I nod, he says, "Then let's get to work."

"Right now?"

"When else? Tomorrow will be too late. The recital is to-day, and you've got a rock solo to deliver."

And so we get to work. I don't have a cell, so I ask Pete to text my mom to let her know I'll be here a while longer. She responds almost immediately, thanking him. He has two more lessons that day, but he cancels both, claiming he's come down with a bug. I can't remember a single time Pete canceled our Monday lesson. Canceling is not a part of his vocabulary. He's the kind of person who's always working, even when he's sick to the point that his insides are becoming his outsides.

But today he's making an exception for me.

CHAPTER
27

It feels just as weird as last time—button-down oxford shirt and black dress pants. Pete's not making me wear red suspenders, though, which is more than I can say about symphonic band. I finish dressing, tucking in my shirt, and fixing my chaotic hair. For just a quick moment, I throw my baseball cap on and stare at myself in the mirror, admiring the casual chaos of my hat against the rest of my outfit. I'd love to show up like this, but I can't do that to Pete. Not after all he's done for me.

My mom knocks on my door, and I tell her to come in. She opens the door with a serious look. The color has drained from her face.

"Pete is going to take you to the recital," she says.

"Why?" I ask. Then I wonder why it matters. Pete's the one who wants this. Why should anyone else take me? But that's when I feel an overwhelming need to be with my mom—I want her to take me more than anybody, because that means she'll be there. Someone from this house needs to be there to witness that I'm a drummer in more than just my imagination.

"Your father is home," she says.

"I thought you were going to deal with him," I say.

"I was going to." She exhales. "*After* you left. It seems he's home early."

I choke up for a moment. My dad went to meet with his friend again today. "Did it go well?" I ask.

"I don't know, Sam, but whatever happened to him today is not for you to worry about."

"What about Brian?" I don't want my brother in the middle of a fight that has nothing to do with him.

"He's at a sleepover. Everything here will be fine. You just worry about tonight. I'll take care of the rest."

I nod, wanting to say something else. I don't get my chance to. Something else happens instead. My face trembles, my eyes water, and my throat closes.

"Are you sure this is okay?" I ask.

"It's more than okay, Sam," she says. "Show Kirkwood

what you're made of. Wait outside for Pete, and remember that I can handle your father just fine."

My mom closes the door and goes downstairs. I open my top drawer and pull out the pristine Vic Firth sticks that Scott *didn't* give me and hold them tight. I haven't used them, not even on my practice pad—the first sound they make will be at the recital.

I hear my mom talking with my dad. Their conversation is in whispers, so I can only guess at most of it. When I know they're both in the kitchen, the room farthest from the front door, I walk downstairs quietly, tiptoeing on every squeaky step. I open both the front and screen doors quietly and shut them as silently as I can, listening to the voices of my parents inside. I'm halfway down the sidewalk to the curb when I finally hear my dad explode. He shouts, and my mom shouts back.

My body shakes when I hear the burst of their voices. I want to run inside. Apologize to my dad and explain everything to him. Tell him it was my fault and my mom didn't do anything. But I remember what my mom said—*I can handle your father just fine*—and I reach inside myself, into the fire my mom is fighting to keep alive, and remember that tonight I will show everyone at Kirkwood that I am a rhythmic tornado—a dynamic force to be reckoned with.

Then I finally see him—his small yellow car *putt-putt-putt*ing down the street. It pulls up to the curb, and the passenger-side door opens. Pete is inside, waving me in and saying, "Hop in, rock star."

So that's what I do. I no longer hear my parents' voices when we drive away.

CHAPTER 28

I don't remember much of what happened from the moment I entered Pete's car to the moment I walked on stage.

What I do remember is streets and cars and lights whizzing by on the way there. Then I was suddenly surrounded by the smelly old wood of the Kirkwood Music Academy. We must have arrived late, because there were already tons of people in the audience and performers on stage. I don't know how it went from being virtually empty my first visit to jam-packed tonight, but that's how it is now as I wait for my turn to perform.

The host for the night calls my name, and I float up to the stage, feeling the eyes of the audience on me the whole time. I take a seat at the throne behind Pete's drum set on stage—his own personal set, I might add, not the one he keeps for students. I might be the first person other than Pete to play it.

I'm the only one playing drums. Every other performer is a pianist, or violinist, or cellist, or some other string instrument that would be much more interesting with a beat behind it. I swear I spot a small group of sax players in the back, but I can hardly see them through the stage lights. Memories of Danny and his father at Kirkwood flood back to me, along with the realization that they could be sitting in the audience this very minute. I push the thought away. I don't have time to worry about whether or not I sound like I'm playing on a garbage can.

I sit behind the drum set and feel my legs shaking. My hands are numb. The sticks are hanging loose in my grip. And that's when I realize I'm totally going to blow this. I'm not ready. I've improved under Pete's guidance, but I still have so much to learn. At Kirkwood I'm a guppy in a pool of piranhas—I don't belong here, and I know it. Drums require all four limbs to act independently, and I can't even stop mine from shaking. I have a big black hole in my confidence, and that hole is going to ruin my performance.

Unless I take one deep breath.

That's right. Pete said to take one deep breath. Right before I start playing. I may miss notes or lose the beat in a few places, but if I take a single deep breath right before I start, there is no way I can bomb the whole show.

So I take a breath.

In.

Out.

And I start to play.

The first note is wrong. I start with a cymbal crash, but I lead with my left hand when I'm supposed to lead with my right, and the whole opening fill is three beats too long and sounds like I'm playing on a tin can. But it's only one fill. And as soon as it's over, I have the whole rest of the performance to think about.

And what a performance it is. Not that I know how it sounds to the audience. To me, the whole thing sounds like I'm underwater. It feels amazing, though, my arms flying across the set and falling into place. I start playing patterns I'd planned, and switch to stuff I didn't plan because it feels like the right thing to do. Before long, I cease to think about what I'm playing at all and hear my inner voice shouting, *This is the best you've ever played, Sam!*

And it totally isn't the best I've ever played. Not even close. My muscles are tense, I hit the rim of the snare three times, and the stick slips into my second knuckle more times than I can count. My best drumming only exists in a place where I never quit and never lie and never hit Danny Lenix with a drumstick (it was a marimba mallet, Sam, a marimba mallet!). But this is good enough. It's more than good enough.

Halfway through, I lose all feeling in my arms and legs, and my emotions are electricity powering my limbs as they pound out rhythms. I release everything—Danny's insults, and my dad's anger, and all the lies and doubts and voices in my head that tell me I'll never be good enough—and swing them into the snare, erasing the pain with each note.

When I play drums, I become them. There is no difference between me and the musical machine in front of me. I am drums, and I am finally happy.

When I'm done, my final double strike of the crash and ride rings through the audience, and the moment it starts to settle, everyone applauds. The amazing sound of clapping hands floods the room. Through the ruckus comes a round of hooting and hollering, cheering and whistles.

I spot Pete in the audience, standing near the back, smiling in a way I didn't think was possible for someone so grumpy. His smile is so large that I worry his cheeks will crack and bleed. He motions for me to stand up, and I do that. The applause rises.

My eyes focus, penetrating the bright lights. Somewhere in the fourth or fifth row are two hands clapping harder than any of the others. A duo of palms applauding steadily enough that their owner has to be a fellow musician. It's the hands of Ms. Rinalli, and her shining face is grinning ear to ear.

She made it. I can't believe she actually made it. I continue to scan the crowd, looking for other familiar faces. I'm not sure who I expect to see. My mom? My dad? Maybe Brian, or Kristen, or Scott and Zeke in the corner, peeing in the timpani.

It would be nice to imagine their smiling faces while I'm listening to the rhythms in my head that will keep me awake later tonight.

CHAPTER
29

Pete is waiting for me in the main hall where students are meeting their families and getting congratulated. He doesn't say much. "Nice work" is about it, but coming from him, that says a lot. A few strangers compliment me, and I can't help but smile. I try again to spot Mom or Brian, but they're nowhere to be seen. It's just Pete.

I see the infamous Pam Stanky talking to a group of parents. She locks eyes with me and leaves their side, heading straight for me.

"Sam Morris, right?" she says.

"That's me," I say. My eyes turn to Pete, who waits silently, watching the two of us talk. "Thanks for everything, Ms., um—"

"*Please* just call me Pam," she says, saving me from having to say *Stanky* without cracking up. "Do you have plans for the summer?"

"I'm not sure," I say, knowing it sounds stupid. "This has been a complicated night."

Pete butts in and says, "Her schedule is open." He glares at me like he's ready to kill me if I argue.

"I want you to think about trying out for our drum ensemble," Pam says. "Auditions are normally reserved for students fourteen and up, but I'd like to see what you're really capable of."

Fourteen and up? I'd be playing with high school kids. I'll need a ton of practice and discipline in the meantime. It's insane. It's scary. And kind of exciting, but . . .

"Can I get back to you on that?" I say, eyeing Pete to see if he's mad. He actually looks quite relaxed.

Pam gives me a card with her direct line circled. "Of course you can, but make a decision soon. You could have a very interesting future."

Ms. Rinalli shows up at my side. She hands me a copy of the program and says, "Keep it. You'll want to remember this someday."

I won't need any help remembering tonight, but I take the program anyway.

"If you do end up here this summer, make sure to say hello," she says. "I'll be here two days a week."

A burst of excitement floods me. "Pam's hiring you? You're going to have a job?"

"On a *very* part-time basis," Ms. Rinalli says. "It's only for the summer at this point, but Pam's letting me teach private lessons to a few students here. I've given private lessons on the side on and off for a couple of years, so I'll make it work until something full-time comes along."

I hope she can make it work. I don't want Ms. Rinalli to have to settle like my dad did. I congratulate her, thank Pam again, and head outside with Pete. Another adult stops us to tell Pete how proud he must be to have such a talented daughter, and as flattering as it sounds, the thought of Pete as my father is just too weird.

"Student," Pete says with a polite nod. "She's just my student."

Pete and I are about to get in his car when another familiar face exits the building. It's the most unlikely one I would have imagined. Danny Lenix. He was in the audience after all. He must have performed with the other saxophone players before Pete and I arrived.

He walks up to me and points a finger at my chest. "You don't think I could be a good drummer, do you?"

"I never said that," I say, wondering what this has to do with anything.

"Maybe not, but you thought it. You knew I wanted to be in the percussion section during the instrument fittings last year, and you think I chose saxophone because I bombed the rhythm test."

I can't resist chuckling a bit. "I honestly don't think about you that much, Danny." Not anymore, at least.

"Let's say I did. Suppose I had a bad day and couldn't even pass a stupid rhythm test that didn't even make sense in the first place." Danny shakes his head in disgust. "Then I have to spend all year watching you and Scott like you're best friends all of a sudden, like you and I haven't gone to school together since kindergarten. Maybe I couldn't have beaten you at drums, but Scott? I could have wiped the floor with him."

"It's not a competition, Danny."

"Says the kid who got a massive round of applause tonight. You think the saxophone players got anything close to that?" He eyes the drumsticks in my hand. "I would have been awesome in the percussion section."

I want to tell him he still can be. I could tell him about Wanda, and hope he doesn't take offense at being compared to an eighty-three-year-old lady. Instead I say, "It's never too late to learn."

"And hang out with you apes in the back? Never! I'm a sax player all the way." Danny sees his father waiting by the doors leading inside. He leans in close and whispers, "For the record, your rhythm still sucks. Do us both a favor and buy a metronome over the summer."

I whisper back, "Only if you learn the difference between a brass and a woodwind."

We both laugh. Not exactly a friendly laugh, but a true one. I doubt Danny and I will be civil to each other by the time seventh grade starts, but at least we'll understand each other better.

Pete is shaking his head when I return to him. "If you're done flirting with Coltrane, we can get going."

It takes me a moment to realize he means John Coltrane, the famous saxophonist. That means he really meant Danny. The thought immediately grosses me out. "That is *not* what was happening!" I shout.

"Relax, rock star," he says with a grin. "I was kidding."

Neither of us speak again until we're in the car. Once the doors are closed, Pete says, "I really thought one of your parents would show up in the end. I'm sorry that's not what happened."

"It's okay. I'm glad you and Ms. Rinalli came," I say.

Pete turns the key in the ignition and drives us back to

Eastmont. We don't say much during the ride. Each of us has a pretty good idea how the other one feels.

He parks in front of my house. I'm opening the door to get out when he says, "You're still in my schedule for Monday at three thirty. Does that still work?"

"Yeah," I say. "Thank you."

"Don't mention it. Just make sure you're there. I'm planning something special."

I say goodbye and shut the door to his car. I take a long look at my house before walking up the sidewalk and opening the front door. My mom is waiting for me at the dining room table. She's drinking a cup of coffee and reading a newspaper.

"How was your recital?" she asks.

"It was good," I say. "I wish you could have seen it."

"Me too."

I scan the next few rooms for my dad, but he's nowhere to be found. "Where's Dad?"

"Upstairs," she says, and motions to the chair next to her. "Sit down, Sam. We need to talk."

I do as she says. I swallow hard and say, "Did you tell Dad about tonight?"

She nods. "He's not happy about it."

"I'm sorry."

My mom takes a sip of her coffee and holds up her hand. "Don't be. Your father is a good man, but he has trouble accepting other people's decisions. Probably because he regrets so many of his own."

I nod, even if I still don't get why that would make my dad so mad. Nothing new to that—I'm never really sure what my dad is going through.

"Did the meeting with his friend go well?" I ask.

"Yes." My mom rubs her eyes, looking exhausted. "He's starting a new job next week. It's not what he wanted, but it will keep a roof over our heads."

That feels good to hear. But I know that's not all she has to say. If it was, my dad would be sitting at the table with us.

"Is he okay with me taking drum lessons?" I ask.

My mom sighs. "No, he's not okay with it at all. But for a little while, at least, it won't be his decision."

My heart skips. "Why not?"

Another sip of coffee, like she's stalling every time I ask a question she doesn't want to answer. "Your father and I agreed that we both have a lot of things that need to change, and he should live somewhere else while we figure that out."

I bite my lip. "So you're getting divorced." My temper flares at the word.

"No, Sam. Just separated for a while. He's moving in with a friend while he sorts out a few things. We both need some time to figure out why this hasn't been a healthy living situation. We want what's best for you and Brian."

I want to tell her she doesn't have the slightest clue what's best for me. Or for Brian, who doesn't even know what's happening yet. But then I think about the recital and how I thought of nothing else while my parents were at home, arguing over how to break the family in two.

"Can I talk to him?" I ask.

"If you'd like," my mom says. "But understand that he's not exactly himself right now. You shouldn't expect more than a quick goodbye."

I nod and stand up from the table. I breathe in and out, multiple times, hoping with each gasp I'll calm down. But Pete's breathing trick doesn't work for this sort of thing.

I head to the foyer and stand at the foot of the stairs. The lights are off in the upstairs hallway, but I can see the soft glow of the light from my parents' bedroom. I climb the stairs slowly. Every time a step creaks, I lighten my footsteps, convinced that less noise means less disaster waiting at the end. I finally reach the top of the stairs and open the door to their bedroom with a squeak. My father is inside, sitting on the bed and staring into an open suitcase.

"Hey, Dad," I say.

"Hello, Sam," he says, still not looking at me.

He's silent for a while after that, so I say, "Mom says you're moving in with a friend."

"Just for a couple of weeks." Finally he turns to me, his eyes red and filled with fatigue. "We both agree it's for the best."

I swallow hard. "Could it be longer?"

"It could be. I want to be a different person when I come back, and that could take a while." He stands up from the bed and walks over to me. He puts an arm on my shoulder and squeezes. "You need to be good to your mother while I'm gone. No lying. No fighting with other kids at school. No sneaking around behind her back. Just because she agreed to drum lessons doesn't mean you get to walk all over her. Do you understand?"

"Yes."

He takes his hand off my shoulder and walks back to the bed. His fingers grip the top of the suitcase and flip it closed. The latches click into place, louder than I thought possible.

"We should probably head downstairs," he says.

I nod in agreement. The two of us exit the bedroom and walk down the staircase into the foyer, following the bright lights into the kitchen. My mom is waiting there, her back against a counter and her arms folded in front.

My mom and dad look at each other. There's a soft exchange of glances between them, quickly followed by hardened stares.

"I guess I'll be going," he says.

"I guess so," my mom says.

I look at the floor. It all seems so dumb. And totally my fault, no matter what anyone says. I want to know more. I want to ask my dad why he's leaving, why the two of them can't figure out how to be nicer to each other, and what I did to make things even worse.

Most of all, I want to tell him how stupid this is. And I don't want to tell him through a headphone jack. I want to say to his face, with real words and real anger, that he's stupid for leaving. But when I think about it, he left a long time ago.

My dad opens the back door. It swings out slowly, and he disappears behind it, the dark night swallowing him as the door slams.

The tension in my mom releases the moment he's gone. She crosses the tile floor of the kitchen and wraps me in her arms, giving me a long hug. "I'm very disappointed in you for what happened at school. *And* about the lying. But I still love you, and so does your father."

I bury my face in her shoulder and try to calm down. It's

not easy. Not when everything is falling apart around you, and you lack even the slightest morsel of power to fix it.

It's weird. Drum lessons are exactly what I wanted, but now that I have them, I feel ashamed. It's like getting my wish has destroyed the wishes of everyone else in my family. My mom says I had nothing to do with it, and that the awful feeling will pass in time.

I sort of believe her.

CHAPTER
30

I call Kristen first thing Sunday morning. I'm still expecting her to be mad, so it's extra amazing when she's excited to tell me everything about her pool party. It sounds like it was a lot of fun.

She asks how the recital went, and I tell her everything I can remember except the part about talking to Danny Lenix. I'm keeping that weird conversation between Danny and me.

"What about your parents?" Kristen asks. "Does this mean they're okay with everything?"

Silence on my end. My breath catches in my chest, and I'm unable to speak.

"Sam?"

Her voice is worried this time. A tear escapes my eye, and I start sobbing into the phone. She sounds like my best friend again when she says, "Start walking to my house. I'll meet you halfway. I want to know everything."

I hang up the phone and walk out my front door, following the same route I've taken to Kristen's since we first met. We're not the same people we used to be, but at least there are parts of our friendship that haven't changed.

Scott's nowhere to be seen when I enter the lunchroom on Monday. I see him in class, but he's even more distant than usual. It's not until band at the end of the day that I'm finally able to corner him between songs.

"I didn't get a chance to thank you," I say.

"I have no idea what you're talking about," he says, his face growing redder by the second.

I pull the Vic Firth sticks out of my bag and show him the fresh dents from Pete's cymbals. A few nicks from several snare rim shots are farther down. "I waited until the recital to use them. They were perfect."

He takes a quick look at them and smiles. "I'll tell Jessica you liked them."

I shake my head. "Sure. You go ahead and tell her that."

I put them back in my bag and take a seat behind the bass drum. I close my eyes and breathe deeply as the booms and cracks of the percussion section lift me into the air and swallow me whole, tossing me back and forth through my rhythmic imagination.

I head to Pete's house after school on Monday for my regular three thirty lesson. I never want to be the musician who doesn't show up on time.

Pete is in his basement when I arrive. I hear the loud sounds of drum cases being moved, so I head downstairs to find him unpacking a brand-new drum set. It's nothing fancy, but it's shiny and new, and that alone impresses the heck out of me.

"What's this?" I ask.

"I'm giving you a drum set," he says.

My heart leaps so quickly that I nearly barf right on his floor. "You bought me a drum set?"

Pete gives me a disgusted look. "Are you out of your mind? Do I look like I'm made of money? This new one isn't for you!" He points to the corner, where the decrepit remains of the old, beaten-up student set is dismantled and covered in dust. "*That* one is yours!"

I look at the set I've played at each and every lesson. I imagine it displayed in my room, on the verge of toppling over from disrepair, but just as loud and brutal as ever.

"You're really giving this to me?" I ask, my eyes welling up with tears.

"Oh, come on!" Pete says. "Don't start crying on me. It makes me sick." He sets up a ride cymbal on the shiny set and says, "It's not a big deal. I've needed a new student set for years. It makes sense that you should have the old one. You can't beat on Calvin and Hobbes for the rest of your life. Just keep quiet about it. It'll be a headache for me if another student finds out I gave it to you. If anyone asks, I'll tell them you stole it. Got it?"

I nod, and even though it will make him sick and I'll never hear the end of it, I let myself cry. Just a little. Pete sees me nearly breaking down in his basement, walks over to me, and gives me a small hug.

"Thanks," I say.

"Yeah, yeah," he says. "Just know that if you quit on me now, my head is going to explode, and it won't be anywhere near as entertaining as it sounds."

"I'm not going to quit."

"You'd better not. Now go home and convince your mom

to let you bring this pile of trash home." He pulls an envelope out of his pocket and hands it to me. It says *Mrs. Morris* on it. "And give that to your mom, okay?"

"What is it?" I ask.

"My official terms for continuing to teach you," he says. "Something we all can live with."

CHAPTER 31

My wrists move and my arms fly across the set. Thumps and crashes bounce off the walls. The bright windows to the outdoors rattle and shake with the vibrations of the nastiest, rustiest set ever.

Brian barges in and starts disco dancing to my beat. His finger points to the air and back, looping within his other hand each time.

I stop playing and shout, "Get out of my room! Mom only lets me practice until four thirty!"

"I was just trying to enjoy your drumming!" he says.

"I wasn't playing disco!"

"I was like John Tramolla!"

"It's *Travolta,* and I wasn't playing disco. Get out of here!"

He kicks over one of my cymbal stands and runs like mad out of the room. I don't even bother chasing him. He'll be back to kick it over again within the hour. I reach across my bass drum to pick up the stand and set it up again.

Now that my mom is letting me keep Pete's old drum set, my brother has been asking her for odd things of his own, arguing that it's *only fair*. Things like keeping a Komodo dragon in the house, giving it free rein the way you might a puppy. The week before, he asked her to install a catapult on our roof and a bin of hay in our neighbor's yard two houses down. Thankfully, she said no both times. I suspect next week he'll ask for something even worse.

I've seen my dad a couple times since he moved out. Once at his new apartment, and once at his therapist's office, where we talked about things that make him angry and how it's his job to work on his temper and his relationship with Mom. I asked if he would ever see me play drums, and he said he would eventually. That made me happy until I asked if he was ever coming home. He hoped so, but couldn't promise anything.

I guess that's all the assurance he can give. I've asked Pete a similar question—how do I know if I have what it takes to be a professional drummer? How do I know I won't starve when I grow up and find myself with no one to listen? He said I'll never know until I put in the work and give it my best shot. Then he added that if I wanted a guarantee on how my life would end up, I should work on Wall Street, because then I'd be guaranteed to end up in jail. Very funny, Pete.

I do know one thing for sure—I love drums. It might not be the headphone jack in my head I've always wanted, but it's kind of the same thing when you think about it. It lets you say something you can't express any other way.

I still hear drums in my head—while I'm at school, or when I can't sleep, or when I'm totally asleep and jamming out in my dreams. But it's not so frustrating anymore.

Because now, when I hear drums, I'm the one playing.

ACKNOWLEDGMENTS

I wish I had a headphone jack in my head to appropriately thank everyone who helped bring Sam's story to the world. In its absence, drum dedications will have to suffice.

I was lucky to be born into a musical family, so a snare rim shot goes out to my mom and dad, Mary Grosso and Jim Grosso. They were my first music teachers, and the kind of parents Sam could have used. Also to my brothers, Adam Grosso and Gabe Grosso, for leading by example and showing me the freedom and catharsis of rock music.

A thunderous cymbal crash goes to Eddie Schneider, a rock star agent if there ever was one. He pulled Sam's story out of obscurity and believed in it every step of the way, including through some rather intense turbulence. Also to Joshua Bilmes, Krystyna Lopez, and the rest of the lovable characters that make up JABberwocky Literary Agency, Inc.

I ring the ride cymbal for my phenomenal editor, Anne Hoppe, as well as Rachel Wasdyke, Dinah Stevenson, and the wonderful people at Clarion for taking a chance on a little book about drums after it lost its first publisher. Anne understood exactly what I was trying to do and helped me discover much better ways to do it. I couldn't have asked for a better place to land.

I play a fill on the toms for my first editor and fellow band geek, Jordan Hamessley, and also Margaret Coffee, Andrea Cascardi, and the amazing former staff of what was once Egmont USA. They were a caring and supportive team.

A rhythm on the hi-hat plays for my numerous band mates over the years, but of significant importance are Erik Iwersen, Seth Koenig, Kevin Scheuring, Dylan Hicks, Ari Sznajder, and Jonathan Beverly.

I stomp the bass drum for music teachers everywhere, especially Don Skoog, who's much nicer than Pete, but just as inspiring. Also to Katrina Shenton for practical advice about recitals and the profession as a whole.

I sound a gong for my fellow writers in the Fall Fifteeners,

Fearless Fifteeners, and Sweet Sixteens debut author groups. Their support and friendship is more important than they will ever know, and a testament to the world of children's literature.

Since I always keep a guitar in my classroom, a strum goes out to all my students—past, present, and future—for the learning, music, and silliness we share during school hours. And to any kid picking up an instrument for the first time and wondering if you'll ever be any good—keep at it, and you will be!

I play my entire set, from one side of the universe to the other, for my wife, Anna, and my son, Dylan, because they make my life rock that much harder. There is no music without them.